BUTTON WILLOW

THE TRAVELER

KIM P. WELLS

Cover Illustrator: Olivia Leonard

Cover Graphics: John Williams

Publisher: BKWells Enterprises, LLC

Clarksville, Mo. 63336

Reach us on the Internet:

Website: www. Buttonwillowthenovel.com

www.facbook.com/buttonwillownovel

ISBN E-BOOK – 978-0-9888626-2-3

ISBN – 978-9888626-1-6

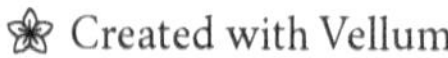 Created with Vellum

For my family; my loving husband, Bob, our eight children; John, Olivia, Christina, Sophia, Winston, Roberta, Conrad and Michaela, and their families. And especially to our current precious grandchildren, Jackson, Solomon, Clarity, Justice, Theodore, Eliana, Fletcher and Evelyn, Chance and August — not to forget the three dear ones the Lord holds and to our future grandchildren including all their generations to come.

May they always remember that God is the origin of supernatural power.

ACKNOWLEDGMENTS

Overwhelming gratitude goes to; the Lord, for gifting the "most grammatically incorrect" person with the gift of story-telling; Family Community Church for their encouragement; My patient editors, Christina Williams, our daughter, JoAnna Mishler, my mother, Paula DeGarmo, a dear friend, Inscript, an editing service; the multi-talented cover art by our daughter, Olivia Leonard; the perfect graphic art by our son-in-law John Williams.

CHAPTER 1

SAMANDIRIEL'S STORY

*I*F YOU WERE ASTUTE and had the habit of seeing with your spiritual eyes, you would not compare me to an aeronautical tailplane. My wings, powerful as they were, could carry me out of sight with one assertive flap. Sometimes I would play. Yes, we play. I have been known to soar within a crowded population and whoosh upward just to turn around and see the reactions of the sons of man. It always brought a smile. However, even though I had the thought to play, I couldn't. I had delayed my departure to the heavenly mansion long enough, for my turn to greet the new Dwellers and share my story had come; therefore, I quickly dismissed the thought of playing.

When I arrived, the walls were shimmering back and forth from transparent to sturdy. All spectrums of light and shapes inhabited by the Principalities and Powers filled the great height of the greeting hall—a wondrous sight and an honorable reception.

Like many facets of the heavens, new Dwellers could transform their likenesses. They learned by experimenting with their newly acquired heavenly bodies. My eye settled on the bag lady. Now, she stood free, no longer bound by earthly confines; yet, her preference still projected her humble beginnings; this told me she would be assigned quickly and used mightily.

Alighting midway between the now-transparent walls, I paused and smiled. All those present simultaneously pulled back a few feet because when I smiled and if I allowed it, my illumination could be awe-inspiring.

I addressed them quietly. "I watch the few who travel, for I am the assigned guardian for all who do. I do not dwell permanently in the earthly realm as those who travel do, but I am often called to assist them.

"I live in this heavenly mansion specifically prepared for those who answer His calling, like all of you, but unknown to the many people of Earth, heavenly bliss is not retirement. We have the divine purpose; mine is to guard, to guide, to push, and to do anything He deems necessary for those who travel.

"The Travelers are uniquely chosen for their gift; all have one trait in common, their *inexplicable imaginativeness*. I call it *imaginativeness*, a word seldom used on Earth, because Travelers go beyond the ordinary imagination, and *inexplicable* because the capability of traveling cannot go before His leading. Though rare for now, Travelers can reach this spiritual potential before arriving in the heavens. The spiritual connection is clear to them; imagination fuels the possibility that time and space are not a finite matter. If it can be imagined, it can be obtained. However, one element to fuel their gift is required: the embracing of faith in His Son.

"One charge obtained the ability before her faith had fully engaged. Even though her conviction wavered continually, she met the challenges the *Ancient of Days* put before her despite her instability. Grace was imputed, an unearned favor toward her. I can say her demands of my presence challenged me, even within this heavenly body. It allowed me to state firmly that faith is an ever-growing attribute within me, within the very heavens. All can experience its increase; this is what Button Willow, an earthly dweller, taught me.

"Now, an aside, these gatherings are for encouragement. Shared stories are an essential part of our being. Their pinnacles leave us no other choice but to worship and fall before the throne of the *Ancient of Days*: Our Father, Holy is thy Name!" Eruptive worship and praise broke loose as I smiled. Glorious light permeated the mansion.

"His Kingdom is coming to Earth just as it is here. We are part of that task. These stories are meant to encourage its resolve."

"I, Samandiriel, the Angel of Imagination, will tell you, the new Dwellers of this mansion, the story of Button Willow, a Traveler, so you can mature in your new heavenly purpose and come back and tell us your stories."

CHAPTER 2

MA'MAH'S SECRET

THE WILLOW FAMILY REMAINED chosen. Father, now the man of the house, had emerged from isolation. He preferred books. However, when he pursued the dynamic archeologist, Mother, he won her eternal affection making her the woman of the house. The books became secondary. They were two opposites of the characteristic spectrum, yet very gifted in their knowledge and craft. Their names ultimately denoted what they strove to be, even with the great gifts they received; their hearts' desired to be parents. Unknown to them, Mother's lineage had the gift of traveling.

The pinnacle of this revelation began in Ma'mah's dusty Victorian attic, Mother Willow's mother. Ma'mah had left Earth to dwell in another mansion like this around Button's twelfth year, and in the Willows' quest to resolve her estate, they found the one item that would reveal her secret: Ma'mah was an earthly Traveler.

There they stood in Ma'mah's tidy attic, Mother with her orderly, crisply laundered appearance and Father with his disheveled hair and loose-fitting attire. They hovered over an old vacuum-seal-encased leather-paged book on a pedestal, wondering why they had never seen it before. Button stood directly behind them silhouetted by the light, but her apparel, her firmly affixed button purse glistened within her shadowy figure. A slim keyhole in front of the transparent encasement perplexed her parents.

"It needs a key?" Mother whispered. "She never mentioned this, Willow. It's old."

"Smashing it won't do," Father interjected, half-thinking aloud.

Button fiddled with something in her button purse.

"Smashing will let the air out too fast. That might destroy it," said Mother.

"Yes, yes, my love - just thinking out loud. Its obvious existence dictates its importance to Ma'mah."

Father noticed the devices within the encasement and pointed to them.

"As always, such an astute eye, Treasure. What do we do? It has to be something specific that unlocks it," said Mother.

"I know," said Button as she squeezed tightly between them from her silhouette. Her lovely medium-colored skin and tightly curled hair always made me smile. Unfortunately, my smile amplified the attic's lighting as I became momentarily visible gazing in the window behind Button. I immediately toned it down before it distracted Mother's slight gaze of her surroundings.

Button had been timid and rarely bold when approaching her parents, so I knew her time would shortly arrive. With a mere gaze, I gave her a push. Her parents stood baffled at her response, querying her with a look.

Button slowly reached into her woven button purse, a staple of her attire, and presented a slim key. "Ma'mah gave it to me on her last visit."

That occurred a long time ago, Button, and you've said nothing until now?" Mother inquired. "We tried to get Ma'mah to move in with us, but she dismissed every attempt. We rarely saw—"

"She said I'd know when to give it to you. This seems the appropriate time." Button sheepishly averted her eyes from her parents. I knew she didn't want to elaborate about Ma'mah's last visit; Button didn't really understand it herself. Trying to explain that Ma'mah appeared strangely out of nowhere remained a task she liked to avoid.

Before Mother got upset, Father intervened. His goodness always kept respectable peace within the family.

"Have either of you seen this before?"

Mother shook her head, "It is quite old."

"Open it," Button said as she handed Father the key.

Mother stood stunned at Button's command. Father placed his well-caring hand on Mother's arm and smiled. His smile always melted Mother's heart. Upon receiving one, she would acquiesce to anything.

Button shuffled around them to catch a better view as Father inserted the key. *Phssst!* The vacuum-sealed package released what looked like a vaporous tonic. The mist sent Button into momentary bewilderment. I leaped as well because a remnant of the Holy Wind loosed within its breeze, so I waved the tip of my wing to push it back toward Button for the full presentation. She swooned heavily, but her parents were too preoccupied to notice.

Mother immediately freed the book and flipped to the first page, blocking Button's view.

"Oh my," Mother whispered.

"What?" Father responded. He attempted to turn another page. "It won't turn. That's odd."

While Button came around, she moved in for a better look. Mother closed the book.

"Careful" Mother said. "How can this most important treasure, except for both of you, be in Ma'mah's attic? Come." Mother jolted the book to her side and made a hurried exit down the rickety attic ladder, leaving Father and Button standing there.

"But I didn't get to see—"

"Come," Mother called from the other room.

Button peered at Father and Father peered back. They simultaneously stated, "She saw something.

CHAPTER 3

MOTHER'S DISCERNMENT

LUSH GREEN GARDENS WITH distinguished flora bloomed over the Willows' country estate. Mother tended it well since putting all her archeologist adventures aside. Planting a garden had always been a dream for her but one garden turned to many. Her landscaping became a visual excess after marrying and settling down with Father.

The Willow home stood castle-like, almost like our dwelling. Of course, ours had a tone no earthly dwelling could emit, but in the brief sunrise of the morning, their estate almost twinkled. The vast foyer immediately drew their guests into a wide menagerie of historical artifacts. Upon seeing them, one could almost hear the personal diaries of those who had interacted with them. Consequently, you could understand a truthful account of their existence. It existed as an awe-inspiring sensory overload, even for me. Mother stayed quite active in her field for years, yet, her vow to give it up for her family stayed a strong one. But, now, that was challenged.

The voluminous library, with Mother's most ornate artifacts decorating it, remained Father's palatial dwelling. If someone offered him a throne in its place, he would refuse it. On this day,

I found Mother engrossed in the leather-bound book, along with reference books strewn on the wooden bear-clawed study table.

"Keeper? Keeper of What?" Mother mumbled. "Nyooo!"

When Mother and her twin sister, Hazel, discovered the unbelievable they animated the word 'no'. It became their preferred response: "Nyooo!"

To Mother's dismay, she suddenly found herself eye-to-eye with Button. "How long have you been here?" Mother bristled as she closed the ornate book, hesitated, then closed all the reference books and sat firmly at the work table.

"I—I'd like to go." Button fidgeted as she leaned toward her.

"Button, we've had this discussion. I'm not sure I'm going anywhere," Mother responded.

"Oh, you're going. Please, Mother. What will it take?" Button begged.

"This is not like you." Mother stood and paced with her back toward her. "You're not old enough."

"What will it take?" Button pushed her inquiry again.

Seeing Mother in contemplation, Button seized the opportunity to open the book without her noticing. Mother continued her studious pacing. Her complete confidence in Button was about to change, for the remnant of the *Holy Wind* pushed her to do things she had never done before.

"All right. You'll need to read every volume in the library first." Mother responded.

"I have," Button responded.

Sighing and in deep bookish thought, Mother continued pacing with her back to Button, while Button turned the book to the second page.

Mother expounded on her contemplation. "We all have gifts, Button, God-given gifts. You haven't developed yours yet. Providence will present itself when and where you can use them."

"I see things differently," Button whispered as she peered at the second page.

"Yes, you have a vivid imagination, but I'm speaking about gifts which are God-sent," Mother explained.

"Father always says the 'Spirit's moving' before he writes. Who's to say my imagination—?"

At that moment, Mother turned and witnessed Button's complete mental devouring of the leather-bound book. "Button!" Mother rushed over and saw the second page opened. She slammed the book closed.

"That looked like me—" Button queried.

"Don't be silly," answered Mother.

For a moment, a standoff coexisted, with each one not knowing how to emote the strong drive within them. Mother hesitated because of her solid motherly attachment to her only child, and Button hesitated because she remained unable to discern the resilient prompting of her *Holy Calling* while essentially obeying her parents.

"Please. I'd like to go," Button whispered.

Exasperated, Mother gathered the book and strutted her way toward the library exit. She grabbed a small bag on her way out.

"Where are you going?" Button pleaded.

"I don't know," Mother responded, as she exited and closed the door.

Never had Button been so persistent with her mother. Until then, she stayed content and compliant, but initiative had moved into her being; approaching adulthood had encouraged her to interact more. Disobedience didn't exist in her heart, only the desire to join with her mother in her coming adventure. Mother and Hazel's lives were filled with adventure, and Button knew the stories well.

Confident in her pursuit, Button raced after Mother. Opening the door, she found herself surprisingly face to face with her. She pulled back and said quietly, "I'd be a big help to you."

"You haven't matured," Mother said as she stroked Button's cheek.

"What are you afraid of?" Button blurted.

"Keeping you safe; you can't go," Mother handed her several very old glowing rebus buttons, "Here, for your button collection."

"Where are you going, Mother?"

Hesitantly, Mother tucked her head down into a hard-pressed thought. She whispered, "Second tier, the third row over, fourth down." Mother pointed at the library.

Button turned toward the rows of books as Mother snuck away silently. "Franklin Dixon, Hardy Boys? Mother?" But, when she turned back, Mother had already exited.

Button stood thinking. She knew Mother had firmly planted a clue; she knew her well. With a glance at the reflecting rebus buttons, Button dismissed their relevance and slipped them carefully into her button purse. A sudden rush to the library's ladder had her bumbling. "Second tier...third row over, and fourth down."

She pulled out a book. "THE MYSTERY OF SMUGGLERS COVE by Franklin Dixon?"

Something dawned on her. "You're going to Aunt Hazel's."

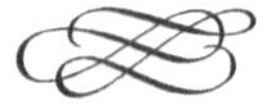

CHAPTER 4

JOHN MEAN

AS MOTHER OFTEN DID, SHE retreated to the garden to work. The worse the quandary she found herself in, the more vigorous her unwarranted planting happened. There she tore into a beautiful flower bed that needed no aid, with the leather-bound book opened next to her.

The first page revealed a drawing of five sling stones encircling a giant who stood seemingly in a cave. Being of keen intellect, Mother had immediately discerned the visual within the leather-bound book in Ma'mah's attic. These stones represented the five sling stones that King David used to slay the giant, Goliath. However, the giant did not appear to be slain or even challenged. The ancient Moabite script below the drawing led her to investigate further, for the second page had opened because of Button's persistence at the library.

Father approached Mother from behind. She always felt his presence before she saw him; his proximity sent a signal to her heart. She pitched her hand shovel into the dirt.

"I have to go," she said quietly.

"Go where?" Father asked. "We'll both go."

"No." Mother quickly said. "You must stay."

"We've decided this," he said, "Remember? No more adventures unless we go together."

"I am very skilled." Mother's rebuttal stood as unusual.

"That's obvious. As an archeologist, you have a house full of antiquities. One day they'll condemn us as hoarders and take the lot. You're missing the point," Father firmly stated.

"This is my last go," Mother immediately answered.

Father's face turned solemn. Mother gave up and finally turned toward him.

"My heritage is involved here," she stated.

"My?" Father questioned.

The one simple word haunted Mother; she hung her head in shame.

"Mrs. Willow, I'm greatly concerned. Why are you pushing me? We're a family. We have individual gifts, but we agreed to do things together," Father said.

Difficulty befell Mother–she pointed to the book.

"This means something." She reached her point further onto the second page.

Father gasped. "It paged?"

There, before them, lay a new image. In the top corner of the page, a young woman dressed in Biblical attire slept at a table. Traveling lines traced her to an identical woman walking about a cave containing numerous artifacts.

"Is that Button?" asked Father. Mother couldn't hold back. Her tears welled, and Father knew his loving arms were the only action that would comfort her. He held her gently.

"I think you need to stay, Treasure, to protect Button," said Mother.

"What...why?" he asked.

"We've always thought her imagination child's play but tell me the definition of imagination."

Father cocked his head while searching his vast memory. His

photographic mind rushed to a visual of a dictionary opened to the word.

"The ability to confront and deal with a problem or need."

"Suppose it's preparing her for something?" Mother went limp in Father's arms.

"Tell me what you're thinking," Father asked.

CHAPTER 5

BUTTON'S PREFERABLE IMAGINATION

$\mathcal{A}$FTER FATHER DECIDED MOTHER should go alone, there occurred a lull in the story. Father fidgeted through every new book, and Button meandered in and out of her imagination. I knew I would need help with all three.

Centuries ago, while assisting the mother of Emperor Constantine, Helena (also a Traveler), I noticed she intertwined with Button on several occasions. Being that the senior Travelers are attracted to the new recruits, I encouraged her future assistance with Button. Thinking Button would be a permanent assignment at some point, I felt Helena could aid in her upcoming transition.

I didn't dare leave Button's proximity now, so Mother's adventure had to be covered by her own heavenly, Geburathriel, the one who musters internal strength and endurance. Therefore, we waited for Mother's return.

Father spent many mornings on their patio steps witnessing the sunrise while viewing Mother's massive garden. As each tardy day passed with no word, his guilt escalated. He anguished; I could barely keep him in tune.

Button, on the other hand, came into her own coping mecha-

15

nism; she resided on the patio's cement bench fiddling with her buttons. They were the catalyst of her imagination. She'd pick up a button, and by her imagination, she'd transform to the historical time or person it represented. When they're young warriors, they know little; time would not be a restraint for her yet; that occurs much later in a Traveler's maturation.

Father had not slept all night. The antique wrought-iron table below the garden steps had been his perch most of the evening.

Connor, their unflappable servant (the story could call him the perfect comedian's straight-man) came out with tea and the morning's newspaper. He tried to replace the leather-bound book with the newspaper, but Father's hand immediately blocked his.

"Tea, sir?" Connor replied to his action.

"Yes, yes, of course. We'll have breakfast out here, Connor."

"Lovely day, sir," Connor answered while setting the formal tray and tea before Father. He poured.

"Hmm." Father nodded toward Button and inquired, "Who is it today?"

"I believe she said she's conversing with Helena, the first woman archeologist."

"They had buttons?"

Connor thought for a moment and spouted, "I often wonder how the Roman stola didn't just drop off. They stayed together somehow, sir."

* * *

"MOTHER THOUGHT it inappropriate at my age to accompany her," Button said as she pulled a Caesarean button from her purse. She conversed with the young, vibrant Roman, Helena.

As I said, Helena's visit remained intentional—to prepare Button for her coming abilities. Button's imagination came about so great and so simple. It allowed her to enter any complex barrier of time and space, a heavenly activity not many on Earth could accomplish. It remained a dream state for her. To others, it appeared as if she were mumbling to herself. One must have faith to see the reality of it but it was real nevertheless.

"I always knew my mission. Saving the history of the Emperor's faith was vital," Helena stated.

"I'm perceived as too young." Button turned away in loneliness, missing her mother terribly.

Out of great concern and the wish to support Button, Helena transformed into her older image as an eighty-year-old woman.

"I understand how a family can appear non-supportive—the feeling of exile. This is my age when I began and succeeded in my adventure. The earth's timing should not concern you," she said.

"Come, Button. Join me," Father called out.

Helena peered out of the barrier Button's imagination had created and assessed her Father. Father had no spiritual eyes with which to see this because of his self-imposed guilt.

Helena admonished Button. "Perhaps you need to broaden your imagination. It should not have you here being sullen. It should not keep you from the Providence set before you."

Father belted toward Connor's exit. "Connor, bring the manual."

"There were many who desired the power of the relics," Helena said.

"Mother is tardy," Button mumbled.

For a moment, I wanted to explain everything to her, but her worry for her Mother would have dismissed any revelation to be grasped. For heavenly beings, our compassion is difficult to contain.

"Button, please," Father begged. "She's just a little late checking in."

I could ascertain her thoughts, but Helena helped her vocalize them with her question. "Why are you so insolent to your father's request?"

Button contemplated, "If I stay here with you, in my imagination, tardy can't become missing, and missing can't become dead. Mother will stay alive."

"You should choose wisely the kingdoms you reside in," Helena advised as she peered through the haze once again at Father.

Father waved his hands in the air like an idiot, mumbling as Conner blew off the dust from the old manual typewriter he delivered.

"The Spirit is moving," Button explained. "He's a writer."

Out of nowhere, Connor placed a glass of juice on the table; Father, in a writer's frame of mind, envisioned it as a smoldering poisonous tonic and squinted. He downed the drink then typed.

"You fill your world with historical personas," Father flatly stated. "By the way, Ms. Helena, Button's mother is the best female archeologist."

His statement became a chuckling moment for me, but not for Helena; she peered heavily through the haze at Father. He had stopped momentarily from flailing to stare at his forlorn daughter, who stared adrift at no one.

"You should listen to your father," instructed Helena.

"But I prefer my imagination."

"My dear, your imagination will become your reality if you act upon it. You're only lingering in it because you are without hope," Helena said.

Father's voice drifted into the haze. "Hope cannot be obtained by imagination alone. Have the faith for the things unseen to be seen. Come to reality yet see them with your spiritual eyes. " Helena raised an eyebrow. Button fiddled with her Caesarian button.

Again, Father's voice drifted in. "Step aside and see it as a gift; bring your imaginativeness to the kingdom of reality. Let them interweave; let them mature. See what God has for you."

Button struggled while twisting the button back and forth in her hand. "But, here, I'm safe," she mumbled.

Simultaneously, Father and Helena chorused. "Let faith in. Let hope find you."

"Promise me you'll try. Come sit," Father said solemnly.

Helena gave Button a reassuring nod to encourage her to answer.

"I promise," said Button.

"I'll accompany you," said Helena, as they both moved to Father's table.

At that moment, a covert principality came with a portion of Mother's story from Geburathriel. I stood aghast to see the principality's light-ray visible to everyone; it even disturbed Helena's mist so that she let out a verbal "Shoo!" I knew this could only be Geburathriel's favorite assistant, whom I dubbed "Little P." He has been known around the mansion as her preferred stealth mode partner. Little P. was generally good in his covert gatherings; however, he thought too far ahead of his task and unknowingly revealed himself. His excuse came about that he remained a very little principality.

"What?" Father inquired.

"What?" Button responded.

"Did you say something?" Father asked.

"No..."

I quickly enveloped Little P., revealing only the tip of my left wing. Oh, my. He had a great deal to add to Button's story.

CHAPTER 6

MOTHER'S INCREDIBLE ADVENTURE

THE CLUES MOTHER HAD GATHERED led her to a magnificent lofty European mansion bathed in the fullness of the moonlight. The structure shared the earth as if it were assembled within the mountainous ledge. Mother easily gained entry through the massive paned window with her expert skills; however, cliff climbing to the fortress's third floor challenged her more than in her youthful days. Her waddled walk on the library floor resulted from the bird-man suit she wore. Even so, she managed to get to the hidden wall safe where she attached some small explosives. With a flip of a remote switch, the safe blew, but so did the mansion's alarm.

Swiftly, she seized from the safe an ancient ornate metal box and fumbled it into a belted bag attached to her side by a carabineer. Something SLAMMED. As she turned, one by one the exterior windows slapped shut and bars followed to lock them down.

"Goodness." Mother shouted.

Her sprint for the last window looked like a penguin in a tight tuxedo about to explode. Her timing waivered, yet she lunged for the small opening. Just when it seemed as if she wouldn't make it, her propelled speed unwittingly increased tenfold. Mother let out a tiny "Woo," not understanding this happening.

Of course, I knew Geburathriel had jettisoned her out the window, so she'd make it before it closed. Mother plummeted the sheer drop off the cliff.

Her descent survived unheard of speed. Mother risked everything; her distance from the mountain stayed narrow, but when her speed gained enough for flight, she flew expertly. However, Mother's over-confidence planted visions of her family before her eyes when she grabbed the hanging ladder from the waiting hovering helicopter. If it were not for Geburathriel's continued intervention, the rotating blades would have snatched Mother's life when her inaccurate grab created too large of a forceful swing. With Geburathriel's encouragement, the pilot saw the dilemma and pulled up to settle her sway.

* * *

THE STORY RUSHED BACK to the Mountain Fortress, with Mother's successful escape in place. John Mean, the antiquities dealer, resided there. Mean happened to be familiar with the Willows' guardians. Evil emanated from him, and evil never went unnoticed.

It was not always this way for Mean, but greed and power had gnawed at him until they left a cavity for evil to enter. Just as with Jeroboam, the son of Nebat, generations of evil made up his family lineage. Within his line, there were times when it would sever, only to regroup after a few more generations. Interestingly, John Mean thought he had no heir; this became a laughable thought amongst the Heavenly Dwellers.

There he stood, a tall man, all teeth, angrily assessing his safe. "The stones," said Mean. "The stones, Nahari. Put the men on high alert!"

Mean's yes-man, Nahari, a gangly, nervously wired man, paced back and forth, not knowing what to do. "Yes, sir, Mr. Mean," he blurted with a hunched scoot toward the door.

"And, get the car." Mean screamed.

Nahari, eyes wide, reversed one step then proceeded.

"Yes, sir, Mr. Mean."

Confused and appearing deluged, he reversed again; then after a frozen split second, he moved again.

Oh, dear, I must apologize. Mother's story didn't begin here. Sometimes, in his haste, Geburathriel's lights arrive all jumbled up, and it is left for the recipient to unravel them.

It seems Father had not been as forthright with Button regarding Mother as I saw previously. Perhaps, in his wisdom, he kept Mother's communication to himself until Button's full maturity could be revealed without emotional entrapment. Mother had contacted Father and Button knew nothing of it.

* * *

ON AN ISOLATED SEA CLIFF, on a windy day, Mother stood before the Mediterranean Sea. The water stood void of any seafaring activity. A woven scarf covered her face to protect her from the harsh elements. She stuffed what seemed to be a receipt into her pouch as twelve cargo trucks headed down the rock-faced road.

Obviously, Mother had made a rather large discovery, for a covered dig with a hoist erected stood visibly in the background. At the bottom of the dig, she wrenched up one last duffle bag. After tying it off, her boot brushed a broken potsherd; upon this existed an ancient inscription. She picked it up, smiled and packed it solidly in her leather pouch.

The next scene I viewed, Mother slapped several explosives on the dig's entrance. Scurrying up the portable metal ladder, she removed her head covering and dialed her cell phone.

"Hello, Mr. Willow. You well? Our little Button? Good. Soon, my treasure. I'll be home soon. Yes, profound pieces." Mother checked her phone for signal problems. It convinced me Geburathriel had intervened.

"Hang on."

Not to be deterred, Mother trekked up the rocky cliff.

"I'm here. Just today? Yes, as I'm leaving the dig, I found a potsherd in the sand. Treasure, you won't believe the wondrous items I've found. No! I'm not just digging. All artifacts I found confirm he is a descendant of Goliath. I believe he's the Keeper; the one of whom the book speaks."

Apparently, it took a long pause for Father to encapsulate the idea. For one so old to be revealed, the excitement, the eager infectiousness of discovery slowed his brain. We knew the Keeper well, and his unearthly abilities continued to remain hidden to the Dwellers of the earth.

"You there?" Mother asked as she turned toward the sea. "Yes, yes, I'm perfectly safe."

Coming about, she viewed the huge yacht anchored offshore; commando-type figures surveyed the surroundings from its deck.

"Hold on a minute, Treasure," Mother said as she flipped the phone on hold then drove her hand deep into her pocket. Out came a detonator; she armed it and flipped it. KABOOM. As she ducked behind a rock, she viewed the commandos' heightened reactions.

After shuffling down the ledge, she returned to her phone. "Sorry, dear. You know me—doing some juggling."

The phone went dead. These were the last words Father heard from Mother. "Geburathriel had intervened to get Mother to focus on her retreat. Mother took a long gaze of satisfaction toward her dig, for she had trucked out droves of ancient artifacts from the Keeper's abandoned cave. This, with the stones she discovered at Mean's fortress, meant she was off on a very dangerous adventure once again, as in previous times with Hazel.

* * *

Geburathriel's encouragement moved Mother, while shrouded in camouflage, to set electronic jamming devices before a Mediterranean Sea cave. The men guarding the enclosure were the ones Mean commanded Nahari to notify. The entrance seemed securely seized by two hefty night guards as Mother crept close by.

"Entrance is clear," one Guard toned on his communication device. He clicked the device twice. "Do you copy?" He motioned to the other guard to try his, but to no avail.

Then, Mother chose to do the oldest trick in the book. She threw a rock to her south to distract them. Upping her game became a prerequisite; old-school tactics wouldn't accomplish her task.

CLANG, BAM, TUMBLE, and THUD. Oh, Geburathriel. He knew the rock wouldn't be enough; he chose to tinker with a rather large boulder.

Sure enough, both guards responded. There's something about blinding light in this story that preoccupied the guards and held them at bay for quite some time. Other Heavenly Messengers were obviously dispatched from another mansion, I concluded since Little P's message wasn't too clear; they obviously had requested playtime. You will discover playing in the blinding light is invigorating and, most of all, fun. I think this light indicates the fulfillment of such a request.

A divine opportunity presented itself to Mother, and she took it. Peering around the cave's entrance, her eyes widened; there, a nine-foot giant sat, stooped over, defeated and chained to a large chair, in front of six commandos. John Mean stood victoriously before him, flashing his bright teeth.

"Transfer your power to me," Mean barked to the giant.

The giant mumbled, "I have no magic."

Mean boldly walked right up to him.

"I am the holder of the stones. You must submit and do what I say." Mean held out his hand. "Touch me and let's go."

Mother's brash confidence suddenly had her standing before them proclaiming, "*I am the holder of the stones.*"

With their rifles cocked, commandos turned as Mean whipped around, yet no response transpired from the giant. He sat there slumped, spent of all energy. Mother could not give up her bluff. She kept looking for some revived element in him; she needed his aid. With a grandiose cavort of the stones' case, her stalling began in an overly confident appearance. Soon her confidence waned, and her worldly game-show-like presentation subsided.

"Get her," Mean ordered.

Mother's heart sank momentarily, but she remained the juggler of all jugglers, and she hoisted the stones' ornate box. Like fine-tuned choreography, the stones dispersed from the box midflight into a perfectly symmetrical oval. Once they began to gravitate toward one another, as these stones always did, Mother grabbed them individually and hurled them toward the approaching commandos. She juggled the rest, keeping them in flight until she had a clean shot. With great concentration, she beamed one commando. Feeling the pull of the other stones, the thrown stone would ricochet automatically back to the oval juggling routine.

"Come on, Colossus, or whatever your name is. Time to go."

This request had the giant squinting with his defeated eyes. Some familiarity sparked as he focused on Mother. "The Moabitess," the giant mumbled.

"I'm looking for some muscle here," said Mother as she plopped another guard down with a returning stone.

"Shoot her." Mean commanded, "Shoot her!"

Geburathriel allowed some of his *Holy Wind* to escape his presence, and it permeated the exhausted giant. Chains broke, and the giant leaped between Mean and Mother. With a simple finger flick from the giant, Mean pasted to the back wall, and the remaining commando handily fainted. The Keeper appeared as if he were suddenly shopping, pilfering some of the military equipment from the downed commandos and tables. Mother convinced him of the remaining urgency and pulled him away. Off they ran.

* * *

TAKING A MOMENT FROM THEIR FLIGHT, they hid from their pursuers in a tall cleft within the rocky beach terrain.

"You're a big target, and my overconfidence is ill-founded," Mother puffed. Her chest heaved for breath as she set the stones' box down and sat on it.

"I serve holder of sling stones," said the giant. He squinted, focusing in on Mother's face. "You returned to me?"

"Yes, I am of the Moabitess's lineage." Mother smiled.

The giant smiled.

"I don't know your name?" Mother asked.

"Brob."

Now, Mother took the time to squint. She thought a minute and blurted. "As in Brobdingnagian? As in *Gulliver's Travels*? Did Ma'mah name you?"

"Have many names, been Brob long time."

Brob brushed Mother's face with his pinky. "She saved me from Pagan gods; now, again she saves me. I call you 'The Moabitess' again." Brob smiled through his own breathlessness. "I am old."

"The Keeper is not old," Mother rebuked.

Shouts were heard in the distance.

"I must go," said Brob.

"To retrieve the artifacts?" Mother asked.

Surprised, Brob acknowledged her with a nod.

"I've moved them."

Surprised again, Brob asked, "You touch them?"

"They were good to me," Mother reassured him by touching his arm.

Brob felt her touch, and his eyes sparkled.

"You travel?"

Mother stood perplexed at his eager question. "Uh - of course, I travel."

Delighted, Brob stood erect for the whole world to see. "Let's go."

More distant shouts interrupted them, and Mother quickly pulled Brob down. "We must separate."

Brob's demeanor changed to its solemn beginnings.

"They're on Andros," Mother explained, "the artifacts, in the Caribbean. Within the blue holes, there's a cavern system. We need to find a place to hide you until I can arrange your transportation."

"I manage."

"Manage what?" Mother asked.

Brob made a swimming motion with his hands.

"To the Caribbean?" she asked.

Pulling out a military GPS tracker, Brob explained, "I have this and these." He pulled several MREs from behind his back and smiled. "I let you know secret: no one eat by me without me taking food."

"You don't understand. The Caribbean is far away."

"The Leviathan my friend. Brob wonderful swimmer. Had good teacher."

The shouts were much closer now. Mother quickly opened the ornate box and pitched a stone to Brob.

"You keep this one," she instructed, "and I'll keep two and send the other two home. That way, no one will have all five. No one can then bind you to the Moabitess's oath."

"But, I serve the Moabitess." Brob pointed endearingly to Mother.

"Then, the Moabitess says you are free to be the Keeper until we meet again." Mother swiftly tucked Brob's stone into his leather pouch. She commanded Brob, "Now swim."

* * *

Geburathriel's story once again came to me sketchy, but it appeared it showed Mother jogging swiftly through a vast outdoor food market, still within a Mediterranean background. In haste, Mother purposely collided with a shopper and covertly slipped a bubble-wrapped package into a nearby mail service box.

Fleeing from something within a dense Mediterranean shopping crowd, Mother's exhaustion had obviously set in. An alleyway opened before her, and she saw the opportunity to step in and regain her escaping breath.

"A bit out of shape, Mother," she quipped, leaning against a building. She managed five cleansing breaths before she zipped around the corner only to run right into Mean himself.

His three thugs advanced, backing Mother deeper into the thin alley. "Where are they?" Mean demanded.

Mother's nature never gave in easily. Typically, her wry smile (a familiar notation known to Geburathriel) preceded an action on her part. She expertly fought the three thugs off and ran.

Mean would have nothing to do with it. He tased her to the ground. After she finished convulsing, he patted her down and found the two stones in her ankle holder. Now, John Mean's wry smile permeating the last light from Geburathriel.

CHAPTER 7

FATHER ASSISTS BUTTON'S GIFT

FULL SUNLIGHT HAD NOW permeated the garden patio. Father gladly received Button's company, and Helena reclined on a ledge of flowers close by.

"You look exhausted," Father said. Button reluctantly received his hug before they sat down at the manual typewriter.

Father stretched his fingers and waved his hands aimlessly. "The Spirit is leading."

"Yes, Father, I can tell. It always does before you write."

"Yes, yes, but my gift ends on the written page; yours remains locked up in your imaginative mind. Let's see what's in there. Jump in anytime," Father said as he brushed the dust off the typewriter with his kerchief.

"Must we?" asked Button. Helena's expression clearly showed Button her displeasure with her response.

Father answered, "Perhaps if we combine our gifts we can bring her home together. The family was the first institution created. It has great power." Fueled by his immense guilt, Father's countenance drifted. "I shouldn't have let her go. We must find her, Button."

"I love you, Father."

The simple words touched all of them. Helena and Father were about to cry, but Father began to type, and Button let Helena go by placing the Cesarean button into her button purse; she disappeared.

Button's exhaustion, resulting from her continuous imagination, left her depleted. She leaned heavily on Father's shoulder glancing at what he'd typed. "No, Father, you're killing yourself."

In shock, she clutched Father's arm, clasping his cuff button. Instantly, Button's imagination *changed* the whole scenario. Father kept typing and chatting, and his voice became more distant, "Not to worry, I can come back."

* * *

THERE THEY WERE WRAPPED in her imagination and his writings. Father's hands shook uncontrollably on his deathbed in the Willows' master suite. Connor and several side servants stood alert, awaiting any call.

The meticulously ordered room contained: the magnificently carved bed frame, Father's prized books set specifically to receive the morning's first light, and Mother's prized artifacts, appropriately displayed in dark shadows of the corners.

Father dismissed the servants with a wave; once they exited, he pointed to his hidden safe. "Behind the side table, push the eye of the tiger." In obedience to Button's hand, the side table split in half, folded forward and almost rolled over Button. There it appeared—her parent's private safe–something Button never saw.

"It's open," Father wheezed.

Button retrieved the ornate box Mother had shipped to him and brought it to Father.

Father slapped a glass off his side table. "Poison," he said. "The letter. Remove the letter."

Button opened the box. There they were: two sling stones and a letter.

Connor cracked open the bedroom door and listened.

Button read: "The sling-stones of David. Lock these two away. If I don't return, then I fear you have lost me as well, for two of the five stones I have kept. Use Button's last gift to find the Keeper. He holds the fifth stone. Give him your two and command him to be free; no longer will he be bound by the oath. My deepest apologies, Treasure. You were right; we should have done this together. My unfailing love - Mother."

The electric moment, hearing her Mother's letter, had Button moving back and forth between her imagination and reality. Within the intoxicating movement, I had to help her maneuver her steps by intertwining my steps with hers, or her imminent collapse existed. Button stayed her destiny, but I could not feel the faith needed.

* * *

BUTTON emphatically tugged Father's cuff button loose.

"She sent a letter? This is true?" she blurted.

"Yes."

"Oh, Father, you should have told me. We could have traced the mailing—"

"Button, your mother is the most resourceful woman I know. Tracing the mailing won't do. It's her clue we need to solve," said Father, as he purposely rolled up his sleeve nearest to Button.

At this point, I could hardly contain myself. Father and Button weaved in and out of her imagination, him with his typing, her with her gift. But the two kingdoms, as Father called them, began to merge. Did Father know? Surely, he had an inkling of Button's future. Had Mother in her intuitive nature interpreted the leather-bound book? I, Samandiriel, knew I would be busy from this point on. As I contemplated Button's beginnings, Father's cuff button came loose and tumbled to the ground.

As Button leaned to gingerly retrieve it, Father covertly slipped the two sling stones into her button purse.

* * *

WHOOSH! We were in the Master suite again. Father's shaky hands removed the stones and handed them to Button, indicating her purse.

"But they're not buttons," she protested.

The connection transpired phenomenally. Father's voice drifted from the garden within the story. Both freely conversed between each world, Father at his writing desk, Button within her imagination.

"No, they're not." Father's trembling hands insisted she obeys. Button complied.

"Show those to no one. You will live with Aunt Hazel and Uncle Lamar," Father whispered on his deathbed.

Button's voice drifted in from the garden.

"But Aunt Hazel isn't married. She's married to her work on the island."

The heels of someone's shoes clicked. Connor's clandestine peeking ended as he closed the bedroom entrance.

"You know I always write myself in with a character...Button." Father interjected himself. "Good. You're moving in and out of your imagination."

Again, Button's voice carried through the storyline. "But I hate the water. Flummoxes..."

From his bed, Father gestured for Button to return the ornate box to the safe. With the closure of the inner box, the side table returned to normal. Father's hand went limp when she arrived by his side. Button knew their combined story stood aside from the truth, even though she believed her individual imagination episodes. However, something fascinating occurred. This direction would put Button in a reality unbelievable by the world's standards. The leading of the *Ancient of Days* could not be stopped. She would succumb to the expected maturity.

From her purse, Button transformed the deathbed scene to a medieval funeral march by choosing a large metal cloak button.

By holding it up to her shoulder, she appeared in a cloak with a large red cross over an undergarment. Taking another medieval button, she waved a red crossed veil over Father.

A fully dressed medieval entourage with the servants as pall-bearers carried Father on a wooden slab. Button led a slow, solemn march toward the door. She let her cloak button drop along with Father's cuff button.

* * *

BUTTON LEANED HEAVILY on Father's side, at the garden table.

"Father, this is so sad."

"Sadness only lightens after you've experienced it. Let's continue," Father said as he placed the Medieval button back in her button purse. With a slight wave of his hands, while handing her his cuff button, Father took over the story.

* * *

BUTTON SLEPT on her single-netted bed in her colorful room under the watchful eye of Connor.

Her room's *Coat of Many Colors* theme fit Button's personality well and landed her the project of refurbishing her room all by herself. The lady's pink metal armor remained my favorite; never had I seen such a controversial piece. Mother swore an original had existed at one time.

Button rolled to her side and out of her button bag slipped one of the sling stones Father had given her. While very focused, Connor sneaked across the room and tried to pluck the stone with his bony fingers, but the stone moved on its own back to Button's pouch.

* * *

COMING PURPOSELY OUT of her imagination, Button looked

annoyed at her Father as he continued to type. "Connor, the proverbial butler, did it?"

Button laid Father's button aside.

"No, not quite. I'm just using him to shape our antagonist. Feel free to jump in."

"A little humor perhaps? Can't you have him trip or something?" Button complained.

"This is serious. Work with me, Daughter."

I stood convinced. Father knew Button would play an important role in Mother's return. His encouragement exposed exemplary understanding. I beamed, like the first sunray that hit the earth, when Button obediently threw Father's button straight up and snatched it from the air.

* * *

CONNOR ENTERED Button's room in a patchwork-quilted clown suit while juggling several covered dishes. "Time for din-din. Time to dine." Connor sang. Magically, he popped a serving dish with his elbow, and it landed on a side table as the lid came off and crashed to the floor. Continuing to juggle, he danced across the floor. "Time to ease the hunger's growl."

My expectations were quickly deflated. Only on Earth can one be so distracted. What was Father doing?

"Father. Father, it's okay. Forget I mentioned humor," Button pleaded with exasperated earnest. Then Father, in all sobriety, tried to type a visual of their unknown enemy, John Mean.

"Who is this man shrouded in shadow?" asked Button.

"He is our antagonist. Look at him carefully."

Father wrote. Button read.

* * *

CLEARLY HOLDING FATHER'S BUTTON, Button stepped out of her

imagination of his written word and blurted, "Caribbean, huh? That's all he says?"

"Yes. It's the one clue I have—a manifest listing supplies that were never delivered. One delivery point for--"

"Aunt Hazel. Mother said something about going to Aunt Hazel's."

"It's what I suspected. Please keep it going, Button. You continue the story."

Button reached into her button purse and pulled out a winged flight jacket button. As Father took note of it, she quickly went into her imagination role-playing Father's written word – almost transported.

* * *

AT AN AIRPORT in the year 1930, Connor escorted Button to an exterior wooden waiting bench.

"I'll check with your pilot," said Connor.

Alone on the bench, Button drew a button of a flight mechanic's work suit. She transformed into Amelia Earhart dressed in such attire. Button stood before Amelia's 10E Electra and waved to the onlooking crowd.

Father, appearing as Fred Noonan, approached her.

"Do you have a mission, Amelia?"

"No, I do not, Fred Noonan. Water can be a great challenge."

"Without a mission, death is a certainty."

The flight suit button dropped, and Button sat on the bench once again.

Out of nowhere, Connor hovered over her.

"All set," Connor said.

* * *

BUTTON JERKED up from the garden table before nodding back

down. Father's cuff button and the winged flight jacket button fell from her hand to the table.

"Still with me?" Father asked.

Button nodded through her unexpected yawn and sleepily moved the leather-bound book toward her. She turned to the picture that looked like her.

"Good. We're getting closer. At some point, Mother went to Aunt Hazel's. We're going to save her. How about that?"

"It would be wonderful," Button whispered as she caught herself from nodding off again.

Father's assessment, thinking that he mastered all this information and began moving Button toward her destiny, failed. He had no idea what she could do. Yet, his heart weighed pure as he waved his arms aimlessly, reaching for another approach.

As Father closed his eyes and laid his fingers on his keyboard, Button picked up Father's cuff button. She locked arms with him, where she fell asleep with her face planted on the leather-bound book.

Whoosh! We were off. Button traveled as if she were Phillip the Evangelist, the first Traveler. She was here, now there.

* * *

BUTTON'S PERCEPTION of her travel time with the *Holy Wind* did not occur to be the grand epiphany I had hoped for. Only aware of it as a dream mixed with her imagination, she lofted due to her exhaustion.

However, Father had a rush of adrenaline that could be felt a mile away by spectators, if there were any. Button still clasped his arm and cuff button, so her journey adjoined with his journey. There they stood amidst a glorious island morning, on a long wooden pier, before a cove on Andros.

Wobbling on the deck, peering through the fog of her exhaustion, Button mumbled, "Father, your realism has improved."

As Father opened his eyes from his first time traveling, the island's visual stunned him. An "Oh, my," whimpered his wimpiest assessment.

* * *

UNFORTUNATELY FOR FATHER, I'm assuming because of his reaction, he slipped back to the garden table; Button's hand had slipped off his arm. It didn't matter if she had his cuff button; she needed only a point of contact to take a traveling companion anywhere. The buttons were an allowed tool for Button to transport because she remained a young but mighty warrior.

Father jolted at his typewriter, assessing his surroundings. "Nyooo," he blurted, remembering Mother's favorite phrase when she discovered or experienced something fantastical. There Button slumbered with her face on the leather page book.

* * *

TIME SLOWED for Button as she meandered down the long pier and enjoyed the colorful flags aligning the walkway. She noted a sign, "Paradise Orphanage: A United Baptist Alliance."

Farther down at the entrance to the long pier stood Aunt Hazel, Mother's twin. Her blond hair flapped in the wind; it's difficult to understand her fixated desire to frequently change her hair color. Why would one want to alter the image given to them? Sheba, her mute aid, stood with her. Sheba's hair, a sporadic flurry, always accented her beautiful bronze skin tone and gave her a sense of true character.

"Sheba, she looks like Button," Hazel said. They both took a long curious gaze.

* * *

FRIGHTENED, alarmed and apprehensive, Father flipped Button's limp arm to his, trying to affix her hold. Vexed, he sat dumbfounded. "Come on, Button." He embraced her, but she slept lifelessly at the table. I felt for him, so I helped—something I knew I'd be corrected for later, but I felt his presence was needed to start Button off. Button's arm suddenly locked with Father's. *Whoosh!*

* * *

ONCE AGAIN, Father stood before Button on the pier just as she pulled a button from her purse. "No," Father yelled, but it was too late. Now he had to play within the rules of Button's imagination.

Button's concentration saw her arm turn leprous, her dress turns to rags as the button unveiled in her hand. Father, in turn, transformed into the priest, Father Damien.

"This is my last stop, Father Damien," said Button.

Outside of her imagination, Hazel and Sheba approached Button; they saw her in her normal clothes and witnessed her unusual behavior.

Sheba signed to Hazel. "What man?" Hazel asked.

Father, as Father Damien, groped for pertinent words, knowing his time could be limited. He stooped to address Button. "Do the noble work your Father has asked of you. Find your Mother."

Button shuddered as she dropped the button back into her bag; Father whooshed away again as Button transformed back to normal. Looking up with a blank stare, she saw Aunt Hazel and Sheba standing on the dock, just as bewildered.

"Mother?" Button mumbled.

"No, it's Aunt Hazel. Button, dear, why are you here?" she inquired. Button's seemingly shocked state greatly concerned Hazel. She gently took Button's arm, "Come, Button. We'll go to the house."

* * *

FATHER'S FLIGHT back to the antique table flustered him. His desire to guard and protect his family happened to be strong, but his presence to guard his traveling daughter came to pass.

He tried to awaken Button from her fathomless travel, which appeared as a deep sleep. Few Travelers had obtained this because they needed all faculties of realism to travel. But Button could be in two places. He shook her and begged, "Wake up."

Button's body continued to be flaccid. Father contemplated, but the answer to reviving her escaped him.

He placed her hand on his arm again and received another limp response.

"No, no, no!"

He moved her hand to his shoulder and waited. Her hand eventually flopped down.

He moved her hand to his head. Button remained lifeless.

Out of Father's view, Connor curiously stood. "Do you need help, sir?" Connor asked.

"You wouldn't understand," Father replied.

"Would it help if I told you I've not understood since I've been gainfully employed?" Connor retorted.

Father brushed Button's hair back, concerned; he knew he could only sit and watch over her.

"I don't want to be disturbed, Connor. No calls, not one."

"Yes, sir."

CHAPTER 8

BUTTON, THE TRAVELER

T HE ORPHANAGE RESEMBLED A typical open-air island cottage, but with Hazel's previous 'employment,' the rustic simplicity existed as a ruse. An intuitive person would note the heavy-duty utility wires outside the compound. Hazel remained the gadget woman. If there was a gadget idea, it could be made, no matter how silly it sounded. It is said in one of her stories that she invented a square mold for watermelon; she bet her adversary she could grow square watermelon. She won her freedom, although it took the entire growing season to accomplish it. But now Hazel served the Ancient of Days; she held her wayward ways long enough, and the orphanage became her life's pleasure.

Faced with Button's unexpected visit, Hazel stood bewildered over the phone she'd hung up for the fourth time. Sheba queried her with sign language, "Still no answer?" In response, Hazel shook her head.

Button and six children sat in a circle in the open living area—an early practical motif.

"I'm Prank," said the dark-skinned twelve-year-old native boy.

He opened his slim neutral colored long jacket and took out a long bicycle horn. HONKY-HONK.

"I'm Chef," said the curly-haired eleven-year-old as he kissed his fingers and bowed. He stood a square-shouldered, cheeky young man who only wanted to cook.

"Pirate," said the eight-year-old Asian child as he pulled out a rubber knife from his belt. "Argh," he shouted. Pirate had lived a hard-oppressed life beyond the limits of his age, but through it, he became a very capable navigator.

Hue, the colorfully dressed five-year-old, began to juggle her vibrant colored scarves. The secret as to why Hue lived at the orphanage had never been publicly revealed. We of the heavenlies knew, but Hazel disallowed it to be revealed.

"This is Hue, and that's Fish," introduced Pirate.

Fish, almost thirteen, removed his navy cap, a staple of his attire, and contorted his face, sucking air like a fish. Immature for his age, Fish's affluent parents left him most of his life on the patio by the pool. He filled his life interacting with the water, and by doing so, he always tried his human limits. A legal dispute with his inheritance left him penniless and at the orphanage; he had a very greedy uncle.

Button appeared to be in a dream state. Reality escaped her; in fact, grasping it became difficult. Her focus wandered to the corner of the room, oblivious to the children's introductions. She remained riveted on the corner, and then it dawned on me like an Italian mother's pat on the cheek. I had become so lazy in my view; I did not notice the Divine Providence of God.

Ayin, the Eye of God, stood almost creature-like, wrapped in a body the size of a twelve-year-old. No one could see him but Button, and other heavenly beings of course; however, Hazel had accepted his whispers in her life, so she often heeded his guiding. His eyes were covered with dense circular black glasses that appeared to adhere to his eyes; otherwise, his complete presence would send Button over the edge.

When Ayin appeared, in whatever form, it meant the recipient of his presence would learn their current state of submissiveness and fear within the Kingdom of God. After all, His Kingdom's law and order controlled the universe. The fear of God is the vessel that reveals the evidence of one's providential reality. Ayin would convince Button to finally grasp reality for she so easily wandered away.

As Hazel and Sheba joined the children, Hazel said, "Welcome to Andros, Button."

Turning to her aunt, she mumbled, "Espiritu Santo."

"Yes, it's the island's Spanish name," said Hazel.

"It means Holy Spirit," replied Button.

Hazel knelt before Button to get her attention.

"Yes. How did you get here?"

"Father wrote about it."

"I received no letter," Hazel said as she stood perplexed.

"A fitting place for your work," Button said as her gaze drifted about.

"Yes, well, we had sightseeing planned for today, a picnic on the near cove. You will join us."

BUTTON STOOD PLANTED on the long pier while all the orphans sat in a flat bonefish boat waiting for her fears to dissipate. Water remained Button's greatest obstacle. It had never been enjoyable for her.

Aunt Hazel offered her a life jacket. Button flatly shook her head. Inpatient and having enough with Button's bullheadedness, Sheba jumped out of the boat, gulped some air and inflated several floaters.

"These will help you. There's a slim chance you'll fall in, and if you do, you will float with these. Come on, Button. You'll enjoy it. It'll be an adventure like your mom and I used to have," said Aunt Hazel.

Button turned to Sheba, "Do you have any more?"

With Sheba's help (she always seemed to be ready for anything), Button sat in the boat with floaters on her arms, legs, and ankles. Her imaginative visual aroused the need for more safety, for she saw herself thrashing in the ocean dead-man floating with nothing in sight. She opted for the restricting life jacket as well, but fear drove her to finger a button from her purse.

* * *

THE BOAT and the orphans transformed into a pirate skiff. Each orphan surrounded Button, pointing their one-shot pistols directly at her. Ayin, unchanged, reclined at Hazel's feet watching them. Hazel, transformed into Bonne the pirate, took the typical cliché stance; she pointed her sword onward.

"Thar she is. The home of the Lucco's. The monster will suck you down to the bottomless blue." said Hazel.

Button peered over the one-shots into the ocean, mesmerized by the blue hole.

Pirate pointed his sword under Button's chin. "Yar destination, pretty—the land of the giants who dwell underneath."

With a wave of Ayin's hand, Button dropped the skull and crossbones button that she gripped. I stood surprised. Generally, Ayin allowed the story to play in this type of situation. He appeared impatient. I had never seen that from him, but Button was a most unusual Traveler.

All transformed back.

* * *

FEAR FILLED BUTTON'S FACE. Stories of giants and water were too much. Hue leaned toward her, patted Button's arm and whispered, "I talk to the giant." Button pulled back with a gasp.

Hazel leaned over and cupped Button's chin in her kind hands. "There is nothing to fear. They are giant fish, not real giants."

Bored with the boat ride, Fish ripped off his life jacket, expertly flipped on his swim cap and tucked his dreads under it. In unison, the children grinned and knuckled each other's hands for Fish's entertainment. Hazel did not include herself in their exuberance.

"The best swimming hole ever." Fish cried out. With a deep inhale, he sailed non-humanly into the air and expertly dove in.

Everyone smiled except Button and Hazel. Hazel's false grin out the side of her mouth revealed her uneasiness. "I wish he wouldn't do this," she mumbled to Sheba. Sheba simply shrugged. Amazingly, Sheba could lipread even a mumble.

After a while, Button feared for Fish. She anxiously looked overboard. The orphans giggled among themselves waiting for Fish to return; they showed no concern among them.

With everyone's attention averted, another craft appeared off the bow. Ayin noted it and glanced at Hazel. Time slowed momentarily for Hazel as the newcomer navigated closer.

Ayin stood and gazed into the water. Fish spouted to a great height, like a leaping dolphin. The orphans applauded and screamed accolades of "Bravo. More. Do it again." Button sat back, both alleviated and stunned that anyone could accomplish such a feat.

By now, the three 'vacationers' in the other flat boat came into view. Ayin noted the boat had drawn nearer. John Mean smiled and fished off its bow. Ayin knew the connection between the boats and their purposeful surveillance. He calmly whispered into Hazel's ear. She turned her gaze toward the two boats.

"Quickly, Fish. Get on board. We're moving out," she commanded.

To add more tension to the story, a wave approached from the distance. It could only mean one thing, and Hazel knew what approached. Ayin quickly whispered again to Hazel.

"Come in, Fish. Come on, now. You're frightening all the fish." Pirate hoisted Fish in as Hazel started the boat and sped off. In her maneuvering, she caught Mean's attention.

Hazel quickly dismissed her squinted recognition toward Mean. He smiled and waved, oblivious of the oncoming wave.

"Hang on children; we've got a big one coming," Hazel said as she piloted the boat on an angle aiming for the shore.

Button completely panicked. Water had power over her. She reached into her button purse to relieve her phobia, but Ayin in his soft voice leaned over and appealed to her, "Try to stay here." Button sat dumbfounded. How did he know about her imaginative adventures?

John Mean dropped his pole as he ascertained the cause of their retreat. He also tried to navigate his boat, but his path purposely went directly for the wave. "Come now, my giant," he said, "Now I know you're here."

Button's lack of restraint grew when the wave line approached. She reached for her purse, but Ayin grabbed her hand and went face to face with her. "Is this what you want to look like?" he touted.

Poured forth into her stood an imagined image Button knew she hadn't created; it stayed forced upon her. There she floated atop the water, fear filling her face, not able to move; she resembled a beached whale with all her floating devices.

Returning to her present reality, Button's terrified eyes widened. Gasping for air, she screamed, "What are you doing?" Never had anyone joined in her imagination, let alone induced a visual. She had no button in her hand.

Ayin had his say, now, he calmly whispered into Hazel's ear and reclined in a comfortable position.

Hazel instantly slowed the boat and swung it around to see. Mean almost hit the approaching wave but, miraculously and to his great disgust, it dissipated.

Button stood up in the boat, a brave move by her standards, and walked toward Hazel while staring intensively at Ayin, who reclined at Hazel's feet.

Hazel queried Button, "Are you all right?"

* * *

FOR HAZEL, the quiet beach in front of the orphanage remained a relaxed place, but Button's appearance nagged at her and got her edgy. Abandoned lunch servings were strewn all over the picnic blanket, for the boys were off digging body-sized holes in the sand. Hazel couldn't keep up juggling with Hue and her scarves. Hue excelled in juggling like Mother did but its expertise eluded Hazel.

Button sat off alone in the sand staring as if talking to someone. Of course, it was Ayin, for Button only saw him.

"I don't want you here," Button boldly announced.

"I see things differently," Ayin responded.

Button flashed back, remembering the same words she said to Father. "What?"

Button stood and waved her hands in front of Ayin's face. Ayin grimaced.

"Why don't you reach in your purse?"

Button smirked and gladly obliged, thinking it would rid her of Ayin's presence.

They both transformed into the Wright Brothers with their 1905 flyer on the beach. Button, in her turn of the century attire, rushed toward the plane. Whooshing past her, Ayin beat her to it.

"You can see this?" Button asked.

"Of course. Let's see; two seats attached to the Wright Brothers' 1905 flyer means this is the return to Kitty Hawk in May 1908," stated Ayin.

Momentarily taken aback, Button stood in disbelief that Ayin could once again experience her realm of imagination. She quickly turned about face and quipped, "I'm Wilbur, you be Orville, get in." Button hopped on the seat.

"Wilbur didn't do this test flight. They made a promise to their father they'd not fly together. Have you ever made a promise to your father?"

Button pulled back. "Very well, then. I'll have a go myself."

"Charlie Furnas was the passenger. The weight distribution must be accurate; however, Wilbur did do seven solo flights…" Ayin called after her.

In her haste, Button took off, the flyer bumping over the sand until the last minute before the beach's surrounding cliff. She flew with a tight turn toward the ocean.

On land, Ayin followed her intently. Squinting his eyes, he tilted his head sharply to the left and the flyer sharply banked back toward the beach.

Button flew over the beach and turned toward the water. "Stay over land, Button," she mumbled, as she thought she truly guided the plane. She glanced at the second seat. There Ayin sat.

"How do you do it? You just step into my imagination. Did Father write you in?"

"I am what I am, and dwell in the realms I dwell. You will learn." Ayin gazed at the beach and horizon. "This is rather fun."

Button smiled and pushed the plane to buzz the beach.

"As I tried to say, Wilbur did seven solo flights before crashing 40 feet into the sand," said Ayin.

Button squinted. "But we're not soloing."

Ayin turned his gaze suddenly toward the sea. "Now you are."

Ayin whooshed to the beach and whispered in Hazel's ear, "A biplane approaches. Take cover." Hazel glanced at Button; she had her arms outreached pretending to fly along the beach. Next, she glimpsed at Hue, and then a quick look at the boys. "Oh, my," she gasped. Hazel steadied herself.

The orphans had accomplished the headless-tanner-on-the-beach trick by burying their heads and bodies in the sand with another's head shown separately from their bodies.

The approaching biplane got closer.

"Get out, boys." Hazel frantically tried to dig them out of the sand. She snatched Hue and commanded. "Dig!" The biplane buzzed dangerously close to the beach. Hazel slammed to the ground as many orphans as she could. "Button, get down!"

Button continued her imaginary flight. However, the biplane

entered her realm. A head-on collision would have occurred if she hadn't slightly tipped off her course.

Up the shore, Hazel yelled, "Dig faster and make your way home."

Pirate had them all dug out when the biplane came in for another buzz. Hazel noted the pilot's wicked grin.

"Go. Run. Now!" The orphans raced back to the orphanage. Hazel headed for Button, who still raced afoot with her arms outreached flying. The biplane came straight at her for the second time.

In her realm, Button exhibited fright. She attempted to put her button in her purse, but it plummeted toward the shore.

"Looks like you'll have to ditch, Wilbur," Ayin said as he unexplainably appeared in the plane's passenger seat again. To Button's amazement, Ayin turned his eyes downward. The flyer dived. At the last moment, Ayin whooshed her out, and they tumbled right before the biplane cut the Wright 1905 flyer in two and sent it crashing to the beach.

A hefty chuckle from Mean echoed through the sandy cove.

Disheveled, Button brushed herself off and regained her composure, but Ayin stood clean—no evidence of the accident.

Button sternly questioned Ayin, "Is he like you? How is it he knew I was flying?"

"He didn't, only I did. He merely low-dived the beach about to cut you in half," Ayin explained.

Button lost her balance from her woozy stance and wobbled to the sand as Hazel approached.

* * *

BACK AT THE WILLOW ESTATE, where Button lay asleep, she almost revived and broke her traveling connection with the island. She rolled her head to the opposite page of the book and swooned. Uncontrollable shivering ruled her limbs.

Father's eyes did not leave his precious Button. "Bring a blanket, Connor," he yelled. Frustrated, he pushed the typewriter off the table and whipped back his hair. His heart searched for a connection; he knew there had to be one, but his worrying consumed him. With a momentary pause, he brushed the hair from Button's forehead. He deeply sighed and closed his eyes.

He remembered Mother falling into his embrace and himself asking, "Tell me what you're thinking." His eyes popped open, and he whispered, "You were right, Mother. Her gift is fantastical. Oh, the realms of the Kingdom of God are not to be trifled with. Let hope keep her between the two, here with us and there with You. Build her faith oh, *Ancient of Days*, so she may succeed." Father bent over and gently kissed his sweet Button. "Bring Mother home, dear, bring her home. And do come back for me."

Connor handed Father a blended wool blanket. Father lovingly and meticulously wrapped Button and rubbed her limbs until her shivering abated.

CHAPTER 9

THE ISLAND THE ORPHANS, THE ADVENTURE

WHEN EVENING CAME, THE orphanage resumed its normal routine. Clearly, Hazel stood contemplatively about the afternoon's excursions. What's happening? Why Button? Her tardy sister had not checked in. She tried to tell herself it wasn't like her sister to visit and ask for a huge favor, then disappear as if to expect Hazel to know what to do by osmosis. They were twins, yet they never thought alike. Frustrated once again, Hazel hung up the phone in the kitchen and shrugged toward Sheba.

Chef, with his apron and cooking hat on, attempted to cook dinner. He hummed "Clair de Lune" and opened and closed several empty cabinets searching for food. Hazel noticed the scarcity.

"The deliveries? Have they come?" she asked Sheba. Sheba instantly signed. "Not for two weeks? My sister would not have stopped our aid. Something's wrong. No one answers at the estate or her cell."

Sheba pitched two cans of tuna over Hazel's head to Chef. He snatched and opened them in a jiffy. Sheba hurled a large frying pan toward Chef.

Hazel conveniently ducked to look in a lower cabinet as it whizzed by, then she jumped up in her epiphany, pulled Sheba to the corner and whispered, "If our deliveries are missing, so are his."

Sheba shrugged.

Chef chucked the tuna in the large fry pan. Hue entered and opened the refrigerator, gazing at its lack of contents. Hazel stared at Hue's boldness; never had she seen it. Sheba hurled a bag of noodles toward Chef, which he instantly threw in the pan.

Hue moved to the fruit bowl on the table where she began to wrap all the bananas in her colorful scarves.

"Hue? What are you doing?" asked Hazel.

"Its food for the hungry," she answered in a monotone.

"Chef is making dinner."

Hue paid no attention.

Sheba sniffed the air and soon discovered smoke rising from Chef's pan. She grabbed the milk and sternly planted it in his workspace. Like Seraphim admonishing a new Dweller, she admonished him with a look; Chef stepped back in great concern. Sheba smiled and pushed Chef's shoulder. This push occurred when Sheba wanted to relay 'No big thing.' She shooed him with her hands as he sniffed the now-blackened smoke.

"Yikes. Milk, yes, must be added to the tuna and the noodles," said Chef as he poured the milk generously, causing the pan to spatter and sizzle loudly.

As Hue exited, Hazel motioned Sheba over. "We'll lock up tight tonight, Sheba. Are my gadgets still buried in the yard?" Timidly worried, Sheba nodded. "My old tanks still in the closet?" Sheba, now fully alarmed, stepped back. "Are they?" Sheba nodded again, this time a bit more nervously.

* * *

AT THIS POINT, Geburathriel's assigned principality sent word of Mother to this mansion. I stood relieved to see the little light ray

—an extremely small light ray. Holding Little P. in my hand, it mustered all its internal strength only to emit a fizzled effervescence to announce its entrance. Geburathriel obviously didn't want to waste the strength and endurance on a more powerful principality, which only meant one thing; she needed Little P.'s stealth capability. For a principality, moving in and out without being seen takes a concerted effort. The mighty Little P. reminds us often that a dweller's perfection is nearly complete.

Now, where was I? Ah. As I gleaned the storyline Little P. brought, it revealed Mother's dire straits.

* * *

IT MAY HAVE BEEN a sumptuous yacht, but John Mean kept it so dim one would never know. There he stood lecturing in his library outfitted with all his ancient collectibles, seemingly to the open air—his usual preferred stance as the man in charge. He held another ancient book like the Willows'.

"I know the giant can transfer this power to me," said Mean as he waved the book in front of Nahari. Amazingly, he had an audience. And even more so, a Spartan flash from Little P. dashed across the periphery of the room.

"My ancestor held his allegiance for many years. I insist on restoring that. That giant is here. Her sister's here, now her daughter shows. It's his preferred terrain. We'll find him," said Mean.

What's this? Muffled noises? Little P. didn't appear to be showing his best covert maneuvers nor a thorough storyline. This made me think he must be behind enemy lines. There were powers in the room that were unseen to him, yet he knew enough to avoid what he suspected.

Mean leaned close to Nahari and whispered, "We'll concentrate on the daughter."

Moaning and muted speech came from the side of the room.

There. The visual came in his message. Tied hands behind a tall-backed chair turned into view. These were female hands.

Mean spoke again to Nahari. "You stop the supplies?"

Nahari nodded.

Mean removed the two stones from his ornate desk drawer. "I fully intend on obtaining the whole collection. They will return to me."

Mean approached the chair where the woman sat tied and masked. He uncovered her face and moved the chair from the corner. There she sat. Geburathriel remained faithful to her task. Mother fumed angrily trying to talk through her gag.

Mean paraded one of the stones in front of her face.

"I noticed something," he said. "Watch."

He reverently returned the leather-bound book back into his opened safe and locked it. Then he laid one stone at one end of the room and another at the other end. Mother's eyes rolled, unimpressed.

The stones jiggled and slowly made their way toward each other. Giddy, Mean hovered and followed them until they met.

"They don't like being alone. Our mission is to make them a happy family again."

Through her gag, Mother spattered, "You just discovered this?"

Mean leaned in close to Mother's face. "I bet your daughter knows where the rest of them are. She's here you know, on Andros."

Mother's shock turned to rage. She bonked him with her head. Mean reeled back in agony as Mother whirled until she blacked out.

* * *

THE EVENING HAD COME to the orphanage, and all were tucked in. Button shared Hue's room, but she remained unsettled. She sat at the desk with a small lit lamp. Emptying her button bag's contents on the desk, she observed them.

"What are you doing?" Ayin whispered as he suddenly appeared.

Startled, Button's unfocused mind tried to take all this in. She quickly shoved her purse's contents back into her bag.

"You think I'm blind, so you hide the contents?"

Button immediately halted her movements.

Ayin reached out his hand and said, "Show me one?"

She handed him a button. Ayin felt it, smelled it, and held it in front of his face.

"An 1851 Charles Goodyear rubber and sulfur combination."

"Amazing," Button whispered.

Hue restlessly moved in her bed.

"Why buttons?" Ayin asked as he repositioned the desk lamp on her.

"Mother collected them for me on every trip before my birth. Some people collect coins or stamps, but Mother thought buttons had a more personal history," Button said as she glanced at one button's reflecting image.

"What's this?" She examined it closely. "Some kind of symbol."

Ayin leaned in over her shoulder. "It's a Rebus button. They have letters and symbols inserted inside. A riddle perhaps?"

"No, I bet it's a clue. It would be just like you, Mother," Button replied.

She quickly grabbed all the Rebus buttons from her bag and lined them up. Symbols reflected off the wall.

"Amazing," Button whispered as she rearranged them a few times.

Ayin reached out and touched Button.

Button quickly flashed back to Mother's letter in her parent's master suite. "Use Button's last gift to find the Keeper and the fifth sling stone." Shaking the image off, Button groped for a piece of paper and lined them up to read the reflection.

"Francis Formal Smuggler's Cove." Button's eyes bugged out as she jumped up exuberantly.

Hue's restlessness quieted her excitement to a whisper.

"She found it. King Francis's Formal has over thirteen thousand buttons. I've always wanted it. She'd tease me, stating she hadn't found it. She finally did it." Button whispered, ecstatic.

"So, your mother's last words to you were a clue for a present?"

All of Button's elation went blank. "No, no. How selfish of me. No. The Keeper must be there. She referred to the Keeper."

"I know where Smuggler's Cove is, but you're not going to like it."

Button peered through the corner of her eyes but could not find Ayin; only his voice resounded.

"It's underwater."

* * *

BAM KNOCK BAM KNOCK.

Someone insistently pounded the front door of the orphanage.

Filtering into the main room, the orphans had various facial expressions. Prank had his rubber band rifle, determined to defend. "No one comes here," Prank said. Hue pressed her scarves against the wall and leaned heavily on them and yawned. Button nudged her when she started to nod off. Hazel glanced at Sheba; concerned, her countenance twisted. Ayin whispered in Hazel's ear. Chef, being sleep deprived, marched toward the door to demand who committed such a violation. Hazel stiffed armed him.

"Everyone, stay quiet," Hazel said as Ayin whispered once again in her ear.

Hazel opened the door. John Mean smiled. For a moment, his hard-colored eyes turned to a natural hazel color. Hazel whispered, "John," but his eyes returned to the coldness that consumed him.

Button stood uneasily. She stepped back and peered at Mean.

"Hello, I represent the Willow estate," Mean said.

"Yes?"

"Can I come in?"

"It's rather late, the children—"

Mean pushed his way in. Hazel glared, about to put her moves on him. How darc hc.

"We are your new supplier. There's some mix-up on where to deliver." Mean feigned his explanation as he scanned each orphan until he laid eyes upon Button.

Hazel scooted assertively in front of him to block his gaze and then blared, "Mix-up?"

Thrusting a piece of paper in front of Hazel's view, Mean said, "Yes, one is shipped here, the other is shipped to these coordinates." He pointed to an "X" on a map. "It seems to put one delivery right on your beach."

Mean edged toward Button.

Hazel intercepted him again, "And the problem?"

Ayin approached Button.

"We need a delivery name and address in order to ship," Mean said as he studied Button closely.

Ayin circled Button as she whispered, "The Antagonist."

Suddenly, Hue blurted, "I leave food on the beach for the needy."

Hazel's eyebrow went up when Mean redirected his view to Hue. She hustled to Hue and led her back to the wall. She stood squarely between them.

"The Willows are very giving people," said Hazel.

Mean responded directly in Hazel's face. "You look like her, Mrs. Willow, yes."

Hazel scowled and threw a strong arm around Mean, ushering him out, "Seems to me your issue is with the Willows, not us."

Ayin touched Button; he forced an image upon her dressed in full Renaissance attire, singing and dancing to a Brobdingnagian ballad:

"It held a secret, the cavern lore.
The giant lad and his trying chore.
Guardian keeper, a pagan's gain,

rests the icons of a holy train."

The household stood rubbernecked and watched Button perform in her night robe.

Mean escaped Hazel's lead and interrupted Button's dance. She transformed from the Renaissance period to the orphanage's reality, looking confused.

"You've seen a giant?" Mean inquired as he moved toward Button.

Like a ballet, Hazel's simple nod to Prank and Chef had defined the intended action she had in mind. Accordingly, Mean stumbled because of Prank's simple trip and stood dazed after his fall grazed his head on the coffee table.

Clasping her purse and her hands, Button realized she had no button in her hand. Glaring at Ayin, she spouted, "How do you do it?"

Ayin stared right through her and once again had several previous scenes flashing before her. Fred Noonan said, "Without a mission, death is a certainty." And Helena, "Choose wisely the kingdom realms you reside in." And Father as Father Damien, "Do the noble work your Father has asked of you."

And in a jumble, Father said, "Hope cannot be obtained by imaginativeness alone. Step aside and see it as a gift; bring it to the kingdom of reality. Let them interweave. Use your buttons to find her."

Mean revived as Button spun around in her remembrance. He whirled her around and demanded, "The song? Where have you heard the song?"

"Hey," Hazel yelled as she and Chef forced Mean toward the door. "You'll not scare these children."

"Father," Button spoke to the open air. "Father, why don't you answer me?"

Prank moved to the door, and with a wink from Hazel, she said, "You can deliver ours to the pier. I don't care what you do with the other." And with that, Hazel pushed Mean over Prank, who stood on all fours behind him. But just as he fell, he went for something in his jacket. Before he could get it out, two dusty derringer pistols were pointed at Mean at point blank distance. Hazel was no one's fool.

The children gasped.

"Get up," commanded Hazel. "Lay it down."

"What down?" Mean asked.

Hazel's stare of death focused on Mean, "The weapon in your jacket." Mean complied. "Carefully pick it up, Sheba."

Like the days past, Sheba snatched the gun and expertly unloaded it. Pirate stood speechless, but Sheba took two fingers and shoved his shoulder and gave him a reassuring smile.

Mean scrambled up.

"Now leave," Hazel commanded.

Button whispered, "Father, I don't want to write anymore."

Ayin responded, "This is real."

Button swallowed hard.

"Start running," Hazel instructed as she cocked the pistols.

Mean raced through the front yard and landed in a camouflaged hole in the yard. Prank giggled. Hazel gave him a non-approving look. Mean managed to muddle out and left the property.

Hazel closed the door; the two pistols went to one hand. The children gaped. "What?" Hazel said. "They're not loaded." She shot the empty chambers. "And they're very old antiques my sister gave me." She blew the dust off them and coughed.

"Sheba?"

Sheba handed her Mean's gun. "There, no more guns."

Hazel nonchalantly but quickly moved to a wall panel and tapped out a certain beat. A security panel opened. The orphans approached, enthralled by it. She activated it by throwing its toggle switch, and instantly, a large electronic hum ensued. She tapped the panel again, and a shelved area opened. The orphans leaned in simultaneously. She inserted Mean's gun and the pistols.

Another tap and it closed. She slapped the wall and the hum dissipated. The orphans let out an instantaneous "Whoa."

"Don't go outside," Hazel explained, "The exterior walls are electrically charged."

The orphans stood dumbfounded.

"I can explain…uh, old rum runners built this building."

Amazingly, her fumbling explanation sufficed. The orphans were at ease, but Button couldn't absorb the reality trying to set in; it had permeated too deeply. She collapsed.

* * *

FOR A MOMENT, Button's consciousness resurfaced in the garden at the Willow home. She spoke. "I don't want to write anymore, Father." Father tried to revive her, but Ayin called her back to the orphanage.

Then Connor interrupted.

"Sir, sorry, if I may, there are some men with a warrant to search the house."

"Maybe I do have a part to play in this," Father mumbled. "Connor, it is critical you keep your eyes on Button at all times. Keep her covered and don't leave her. I'll be back."

"Yes, Sir."

CHAPTER 10

SOLVING MOTHER'S MYSTERY

$\mathcal{I}$N THE WEE HOURS OF THE NIGHT, Ayin observed Hazel scrambling in a closet. Sensing a presence, Hazel turned around and scanned the room up and down. Nothing appeared noticeable, but she knew this feeling. A divine presence pressed her. She looked up at the ceiling and smiled.

* * *

HUE HAD AWAKENED, if you could call it an awakening; sleep-walking ensued. She snuck the fruit snack she had wrapped and hidden under her pillow and passed Button as she slept.

* * *

HAZEL DOUBLE-CHECKED her old scuba gear when Hue passed her, heading for the front door. Dropping her tank with a CLANG, Hazel grabbed Hue away from the exit.

"Hue, where are you going? Hue. The outside walls!"

Dazed and bewildered, Hue stood looking up at Hazel.

"It's okay, Hue, come on back to bed." Hazel led her past Ayin as she spoke toward the ceiling, "We cannot ignore this."

As she left the room, Ayin stated, "I suppose not."

* * *

THE FULL MOON's radiant light on the beach aided Hazel's equipment check but left little cover for covert action. She attached several gadgets to her scuba belt.

A couple of pat-downs for different pieces—a giant flashlight, and a portable air device—a big breath and she's set. She scanned the ocean waves.

Ayin stood on a wave smiling toward Hazel.

"I wish my sister were here." She breathed in deeply. "One hour and I'll return. They won't even know I've gone."

She walked awkwardly into the ocean and immediately tripped over her fin. SPLAT. Down she went.

"Maybe two hours." She gathered herself and dove in.

* * *

KIND, compassionate little Hue couldn't refrain from delivering her morsel offering, even in her sleep. She took the food tied in a scarf from under her pillow and walked as if she were on a cloud toward her creaky bedroom door. Button arose just as she exited.

"Hue?" Button said as she quickly tied her button purse around her waist.

Ayin interceded at the main door; he waved his hand over the security area in the wall, and the hum of the electronics ceased.

Wanting to protect her, Button rushed after Hue toward the exterior wall panel, but she noted the hum had disappeared. Catching a glimpse of Hue going out the front door, Button understood her destination had a purpose.

At the beach, Hue delicately laid her scarf-tied treat on the softest sand. There lay the tiniest yet blessed morsel. Because of

Hue's vulnerability, I assisted her emotionless walk back to the orphanage; Hue's hair wisped Button's shoulder as she went sending an overwhelming sense of holiness through Button.

"Aw, Hue, who are you feeding? So sweet." Button turned to confront her before her departure, but instead, Ayin stood right in front of her. He prevented Button from visually seeing us for Hue slept in my lap momentarily before I encouraged her to sleepwalk home.

"Ayin," she screeched, holding her button purse close to her. "You startled me."

"Sh. We're not alone," he responded.

Lights zigzagged up and down the beach. Button clung to her button bag, about to reach in.

"No time for that. This way," Ayin whispered as he tugged her to follow. They ran for the long pier.

Button looked back and saw the flashlights concentrating on Hue's gift.

"He'll be here," Mean said.

Alerted by Button's footsteps on the pier, the flashlights whipped back and forth trying to catch a view of who caused the noise. Of course, Ayin's footsteps were not heard; he kept his anonymity before anyone except Button.

At the pier's end, Button panicked. "There's no way out. You led me here only to be trapped."

"There's always a way out."

Button gawked over the pier's edge seeing the water. "I can't," she cried.

"You must."

Instantly, Mean and his crew's flashlights concentrated on Button's face, blinding her.

"My dear, don't be afraid," Nahari cooed.

Button mustered the little courage she had. "Go away," she driveled.

"To see your mother again, you must give me the stones," said

Nahari as he stepped between the lights and Button. His tall, skinny silhouette was all Button could make out.

"Mother's alive?"

Mean's silhouette appeared as well, "We need the stones to free her."

A slight breeze whooshed over Button. She remembered her father's words, "Show them to no one."

"Stones? I don't have any stones."

Mean stepped forward and signaled his men to lower the light beams, and then Button saw the full force confronting her. Mean knew Button had help and he'd have to act fast. No breeze came without purpose. He held out his two stones. Nahari stepped forward. Button backed as far as she could before she hit the rail's edge.

Then, with the strong pull of the stones, Button's purse reached for Mean's stones. Mean smiled his insipid grin—the one thing he stayed known for. Button flung herself on the railing, grasping with all her might. But the strong pull replaced the gravity controlling Button's feet, and they lifted. Mean did all he could to hold on to his stones as well. When Button clung horizontally to the deck, Mean slid forward. Ayin had to step between them.

Aghast, Mean distinguished the faint image of Ayin. Button did have help. With Ayin's intercession, Button's feet plopped down to the deck.

"Get her," Mean commanded.

Shocked, Button propelled over the railing with the slight thought that Ayin had hurled her over, but he remained nowhere to be seen.

Mean's bullies rushed the edge so fast two of their flashlights fell into the water.

Fear consumed Button as she thrashed the water furiously. "Ayin," she screamed.

"She can't swim," Mean deduced. "Nahari, after her or we'll lose the stones."

Indecisive, yet under pressure, Nahari awkwardly dove in. He swam toward Button; he saw her go under, then back up again.

"Ayin?" Button screamed, "Where are you?"

"Hang on." Button only heard Ayin's voice. He had taken an unseen stance in front of Mean to prevent him from sending in his whole crew. Being always ready, I caught the slight movement of his index finger toward me.

Button searched left and right and saw Nahari's approach. "No, no." She looked down into the water. "Something's got me." Before she could utter another word, something pulled her straight down just as Nahari tried to nab her.

Nahari squealed like a dying pig. "There's something in the water. The Lecous." His thrashing panic propelled him back toward the pier.

What no one realized, I took the opportunity given to assist Button by drawing her down with a force the awaiting Hazel could not have produced. Hazel had returned early and saw Button's predicament from underwater. With my pull, she simultaneously fitted Button with the extra breathing apparatus that she had strapped to her belt; all went well. Hazel towed Button deep into the water unseen.

Mean searched with his flashlight, and a far-off wave caught his eye.

"Nahari, get out of there. Stand down men, lights off," Mean commanded.

Just as Nahari made it to the pillars of the pier, water spewed up like a large fountain. As the water dispersed, Brob stood under the one light shining; it was Mean's flashlight.

Brob gasped a deep breath then belched loudly. Loud hiccups immediately followed. While pounding his chest to rid himself of the annoying spasms, Brob noticed the small light beam on his hand. He turned. "Huh?" He scanned the pier. The flashlight went off.

Brob turned back to the shoreline, and again he noticed the light beam on his chest. He whipped around again to the pier. The flashlight went off.

Obviously, Brob lacked his full capacity. He rubbed his swollen eyes and pink-cheeked face, shook himself clumsily and sloshed toward the beach.

Mean's flashlight beam waggled on Brob's cheeks.

"Aaaaahhhhhh," Brob belted as he stormed the pier. Before he arrived, the flashlight dropped in the water and floated.

Brob could not see Mean through his drunken stupor, and Mean's men were hidden in the shadows of the pier.

He resigned to slosh through the shallows toward the beach again. Brob's feet thumped heavily as he took a wide stride, focusing on the shoreline. No drunken sailor exiting a pub could match it. His massive hands untied the tiny morsel from Hue's scarf. He swallowed it as if it were his last meal then tucked Hue's scarf under his belt. Ga-thump, Ga-thump, Brob made his way back to the shallows. Hiccup. Hiccup. He groaned and searched the shallows. "Here, fishy fishy," he whispered. He slapped the water; a large fish flopped up. He nabbed it as Mean scuffled his feet down the pier to get a closer look.

Brob waded nonchalantly closer to where he heard the footsteps. Mean hit the deck, frozen. After a few more waded steps, Brob managed to focus through his drunkenness on John Mean. "Huh?"

Mean smiled. Abruptly, without a thought, Brob took his only food source and hurled the fish at Mean. The fish packed a wallop and Mean slid to the end of the pier.

* * *

AT ABOUT THAT MOMENT, a terrible time for the interruption, Geburathriel had sent another light message. He had been delayed because his instructions were to watch Father.

Father's visitors were getting impatient. His 'guests' had taken advantage when Father had momentarily stepped out of his vast library. They hurled items everywhere in search for clues to the whereabouts of the stones.

Stealthily clicking off his cell phone, Father re-entered the room. He stepped over a pile of books and reached down for the title *Sir Robert's Book on Self-Defense* lying haphazardly on the floor. He flipped through its pages and absorbed its full contents; this remained Father's unique gift.

"Gentlemen," The men stopped their fury. "Your credentials could not be verified. What are you looking for?"

It became a staring game, with everyone waiting for someone to make the next move. It appeared one man went for a gun, and Father hurled the book at it; the pistol zoomed across the floor. All the men went for the gun, and then the light message fizzled out.

CHAPTER 11

BUTTON EMBRACES HER GIFT

A LIGHT GLISTENED BENEATH the underwater ledge (the only access to the island's elaborate caves). Hazel surfaced and tossed her flashlight to the ledge's floor line. Exhausted and frantic for breath, Button slapped at her mouthpiece with her chest heaving, while Hazel hoisted Button to the dry cave's floor. Boosting herself up, Hazel quickly removed her tank and took the portable air unit out of Button's mouth.

Button hacked heavily, attempting to rid her lungs of the water she inhaled. Hazel flipped her on her side, "That's right, get it out."

Button moaned and rubbed her eyes. "My eyes."

"Keep them closed for a while."

In a visual haze, Button beheld Hazel. "Mother?"

"No, dear. It's me, Aunt Hazel. I took you from the beach to here. You're safe now."

"Where are we?" Button asked.

With a perky smile, Hazel replied, "On an adventure." Hazel rose and grabbed the flashlight while Button still moaned.

There it stood, the toggle switch; Hazel threw it upward. The cave illuminated in soft light as Hazel inspected the south wall.

"Your mother and I went on a lot of adventures when we were

young. Long ago, long before I came here to do the Lord's work. Not that our adventures weren't the Lord's work." Hazel turned back. Button stood dumbfounded.

"I begged to go with Mother, but she wouldn't have it," mumbled Button.

In bewilderment and awe, Button scanned the artifacts embedded within the cave's walls. Old crocks lay broken on the floor. "What's that smell?"

Hazel examined the crocks. "Rum. Old rum crocks. He must be starving to resort to this."

"Who?"

Hazel returned to Button's side. "Hmm. Where to start? Your mother sent these artifacts about a month ago."

"When she went missing?" Button replied.

"Missing?" asked Hazel.

"You didn't know?" Button asked.

Concerned, Hazel replied, "Since you arrived, I've been trying to get ahold of your parents without success." Hazel hugged Button. "Dear sweet child. I will get to the bottom of this."

"Why are we here?"

"Your mother sent the artifacts here for safe keeping. The Keeper came a week after she unloaded them."

Under her breath, as she scanned the cave, Button whispered, "The Keeper."

Hazel gazed around. "But there's a lot more than this."

"You know the Keeper?"

Button examined an artifact as Hazel came beside her. Button murmured, "I know this one. The Machine of the Ancient Wise Ones. This used to measure the stars, sun, moon, and planets."

"Yes," Hazel responded, "It showed the ancient mariners how to sail the oceans of the world."

Button reached to touch the machine, but Hazel quickly pulled her hand away. "I wouldn't touch it," Hazel strongly warned.

"It looks like a simple cross," Button responded.

"Not a coincidence, I'm sure. Button," Hazel pulled her aside, "did you see the book in Ma'mah's attic?"

"Yes."

"Your mother explained that it told of a Moabite woman of great affluence. We are direct descendants of hers. After King David fought the giant Goliath with his sling stones, Goliath's family was pursued. A certain nephew refused to worship the pagan gods and experienced salvation with a Moabitess who knew the Lord. She hid him with a purpose, to be the keeper of the artifacts. Button, your mother is doing the same thing today."

"I don't understand." Button paced until Ayin interceded behind her.

"Open your eyes, Button," Ayin said.

Button whirled around, "You."

Hazel squinted; she scanned for another.

"The rebus buttons, this is the place."

Hazel inquired, "Who are you talking to?"

Button raised her voice and proclaimed loudly, "You pushed me off the dock."

Perplexed, Hazel asked, "What are you saying? It certainly wasn't me."

Facing Hazel, "Not you." Now Button faced Ayin. "Him. Ayin did."

"Who?" Hazel asked.

Ayin inquired, "Are you ready for this?"

Button suddenly examined her surroundings with a seriousness Hazel hadn't seen before. Hazel stood concerned.

Button faced Ayin, "Why hide them?"

"Man is hungry for their power," Ayin stated as he faded away and then disappeared completely.

Button whipped around yet didn't see him.

Hazel approached the exasperated Button. "Your mother and the Keeper hid them because men seeking these can be ruthless and dangerous. The relics are powerful. The labyrinth of caves is vast here. The Keeper probably utilized them all."

Wearied and deeply emotional, Button asked, "Is that what happened to Mother? Did these men kill her?"

"Heaven forbids."

Button sulked and leaned heavily on the cave's wall.

"Mother was right, I'm not ready."

"When the Keeper came—" Hazel started.

"Keeper, what is a Keeper?"

Without any warning, Brob exploded over the water's ledge and slid across on the cave floor sloshing like a wet penguin.

"Weeeeeeee!"

Brob's landing stopped at the feet of Button and Hazel.

Horrified, Button screamed.

Also horrified to see people in his cave, Brob let out a resounding bellow.

* * *

SHEBA WATCHED the coffee table rattle as Brob's scream reverberated. She glanced toward the window where she made out an inkling of light. Walking up to the window, she saw boats in the bay. Lights flashed all over the beach.

Prank and Pirate entered.

"What is that?" Prank asked.

Brob's scream ended.

Sheba pointed to the window.

* * *

FRIGHTENED, Button retreated as Hazel moved in to assess Brob.

Through his drunken stupor, he focused on Hazel. "Hello, holy lady." He half smiled before he passed out.

Hazel knelt to feel Brob's head. "This is the Keeper. Brob, the descendant of Goliath."

Terror seized Button as she reached into her button purse for an expected escape.

"Poor thing must be half starved to resort to century-aged rum. Wake up, Brob."

Button stood with a fist full of buttons.

* * *

WHOOSH! Button stood on a battlefield with the Continental Army line, facing the British.

A captain of the regiment commanded, "Ready. Aim."

* * *

CONNOR ADJUSTED the blanket over Button just as she disappeared. He raised a curious, calm eyebrow as he examined the empty blanket.

Behind him, through the multi-paned window, stood the silhouette of Father and the two desperate men holding the gun high above them, struggling for possession.

* * *

WHOOSH! Button sat as Clara Harris next to Mary Todd Lincoln in Ford's theatre.

Mary Todd leaned over to the President and whispered, "What will Miss Harris think of my hanging on to you so?"

"She won't think anything—"

Button stood and shouted, "No."

A gunshot resounded.

* * *

TO CONNOR'S ASTONISHMENT, Button re-appeared in her sound sleep state. He looked behind to the paned window and saw Father as he leaped off the library ladder and hook-kicked the two men. Connor knew his instructions—not to abandon Button.

* * *

BACK AT THE CAVE, Button spilled her handful of buttons on the cave floor.

She didn't realize the whirlwind of her imagination pointed to a clear path for her to take. An unimaginable puzzle opened to her —a puzzle with no corners or color references. Her mind overloaded.

Hazel leaned heavily over Brob, very concerned. "Come on, wake up."

Button whispered, "This can't be real."

Ayin's voice reached into her mind. "Touch him."

Button's expression resembled a human calculator desperately trying to make sense of an equation. She hesitantly approached Brob, knelt and picked up a button next to him, simultaneously touching him. Button slumped over with her eyes closed.

"Yes, of course. Prayer is best in these times. You're quite right," said Hazel as she closed her eyes and sat next to Brob.

Whoosh! Brob and Button were swept away by the *Holy Wind*.

* * *

AS CONNOR READJUSTED Button's blanket again, she completely disappeared. He shot to a standing position, "I'm flabbergasted. Just flabbergasted."

He glanced back to the paned window to see Father. With super-strength Father flattened two of the men by whirling one into the other, then, he hurled and hurled the remaining one. Father brushed off his hands in satisfaction.

* * *

BUTTON OPENED her hand and gazed at the unique button she held, and then noticed her surroundings had changed. She sat at an outdoor cafe table across from Brob; Brob sat on the ground with his head below the umbrella.

A waitress with the same buttons on her uniform hesitantly placed one large mug of coffee on the table.

"It's you who travels," Brob said as he tilted the umbrella away from his face.

"Here, you need this," Button said groggily as she pushed the coffee toward him.

A full tray of food went by. Brob nosed it. Button instinctively grabbed it away from the waitress.

"Please, he's starving. And bring more."

The waitress gaped and backed off.

With one gulp, Brob finished the whole tray while the customers eyeballed them. They had encircled them echoing their "oohs".

"Lots more. Bring lots more," said Button.

The waitress dropped her jaw and backed away again. Customers approached the sidewalk cafe and added themselves to the circle of onlookers.

Brob's reach went over the crowd and snatched food from the nearby customers' plates. He lacked all social graces and mumbled with his mouth full. "The Moabitess could be in two places at once," he said. "She traveled. You travel."

"So, you're saying I'm really here."

He nodded, and he smacked down another stolen plate.

"Mind your manners," she whispered.

"She traveled on the *Holy Wind*. You're here and in the cave. You whooshed me here," Brob muttered as an elderly woman slapped his hand before he took her chicken dinner.

"Sorry, Lady."

* * *

HAZEL MUMBLED her prayers for Brob not noticing he no longer laid on the cave floor beside her. Still, Button slumped to the ground with a humble appearance of prayer.

* * *

AT THE WILLOW ESTATE, Connor finally had enough of Button's oddities. He squeaked out a phrase like he had just begun puberty. "Sir, there's something you should see. Rather, not see. Sir?"

Button had disappeared.

* * *

AN EPIPHANY STRUCK BUTTON. "I started at home. I'm no longer at home. You said two places."

Brob managed a nod as he grabbed another passing tray of croissants.

"We need to go." She reached for Brob's arm.

"How do I do it?" Button asked.

"I dunno."

Button mustered a determined squint trying to move within her own power.

Three waiters came up with trays of food to occupy Brob, while other waiters tried to scramble the crowd. He shoved food down his throat.

"Perhaps I need a willing partner."

Brob gulped his last croissant and sighed. Button squeezed his arm. Nothing. Button stared at the locked arms of the waiters holding back the crowd.

"Relax, it come," Brob said. "I help." Brob stood to his full height and as soon as the chorus of "oohs" started he *roared*. The tabled bounced and the people were blown away at the force. Sitting down calming, Brob smiled at Button as he let go of her once she felt the ground again. She too was blown horizontally yet only momentarily.

"Where were you first time?" Brob asked.

Button was so beguiled she did not understand his question.

"The first time you traveled."

"I feel asleep. I was asleep at home." Button sat down with a big cleansing breath...*Whoosh!*

* * *

BUTTON REAPPEARED and promptly sat erect at her resting place at the home estate. Brob huddled as best he could on the ground beside her. Connor stood startled; nothing audible came from his lips. He eyed Brob from his frozen position.

Behind them, visible through the latticed window panes, Father launched books at his one remaining opponent. One book, however, caught his eye, and he paused for a second to absorb it: *ALI: BOXING MEMORABILIA.*

Trying to break with his usual shocked and stunned introduction, Brob simply said "Hello" to Connor.

"Connor, where's Father?" Button asked a bit woozy from her traveling.

Connor rose, then Brob rose to full height and reassured him, "I am friend."

Connor's stance weaved.

"Bend knees, it helps," Brob recommended.

"Father? Where's Father?" Button grabbed the table for her balance.

Connor pointed toward the library windows. "Inside with authorities."

"Tell him I need him. Tell him I found the Keeper. Quickly, Connor."

"Certainly, I'll just go—" he turned toward the house bumbling, "tell your father, you've disappeared and reappeared, and you have a very large friend."

Father danced and waved his opponent forward, all in grand Ali style. PUNCH, DODGE, JAB.

As Connor reached the entrance, the final foe crashed through the window after encountering Father's final punch. The man sprawled before Connor's feet. Father danced in celebration, fully consumed with his victory. "Great, great. That was the greatest."

Connor took a calm step over the downed man and said, "Sir?"

Grasping for the words to say, Connor turned around, and there Brob stood in his great height behind him.

The downed man managed to his feet. He wobbled between Brob and Connor, not fully conscious of his surroundings. Connor assessed him; Brob assessed him. Finally, Brob said, "Be my guest." Connor managed a sly smile and flicked the man with a finger, and the false authority slumped to the ground.

Father stepped out of the broken glass, brushing himself off while eyeing a book in his hand. "I am not the greatest, yet I feel exuberant. Connor, call the real authorities and see that these men are incarcerated—"

Father thumped right into Brob. He slowly eyed his physique from his hip up. "Oh, my."

"Father, we need to go."

"Button, you're here."

"Father!"

"Go where?"

"To Aunt Hazel's."

Assessing Brob, Father said, "I guess I could get some tickets, hire a private jumbo."

"No, not that way." Button seized them both, Brob and Father, and dragged them back to the table. She laid her head on the leather-bound book. "This way."

Nothing happened.

"Come on," Button complained.

"Button—" Father couldn't manage a single word for they all whirled away. *Whoosh!*

Connor resumed his original orders and covered the sleeping Button. He didn't attempt to comprehend or respond to Father and Brob's disappearance. He was content with his task.

CHAPTER 12

MEETING THE KEEPER

OF COURSE, BUTTON STAYED new to traveling. Her control, or what she thought she could control, had not been fully established. It's limitless in space and time; a lightly weighted feeling of freedom yet with a destination always determined by the Holy Wind. When she experienced it as a youth within her imagination, the Holy Wind would allow her to travel on her own initiative for a while; however, the Holy Wind remained sovereign. So, it surprised Button, as she descended upon the beach in front of the orphanage, that her grip on Father unexpectedly released. Her control had limits. They were still a good distance above the ground (Brob stood tip-toeing through the sand) when Father tumbled and somersaulted, landing flat on his back. Brob and Button, on the Holy Wind, ascended in Father's full view and disappeared.

They revived in the cave just as Hazel finished praying.

Without a glance toward the ocean, Father shot up and headed toward the orphanage.

There were boats in the cove. Three boats...

* * *

Brob lay smiling at Button as her eyes darted back and forth searching for her father.

"Father?" Button called out loudly.

"The orphans need help," Ayin said.

"How do you fit in all of this?"

Hazel stood up from her prayerful kneeling, bewildered as she watched Button talk to the air. "Who are you talking to, Button?"

Brob stood to full height, "He is here. Sometimes you see, sometimes you don't."

"Sounds like God," Hazel mumbled.

Ayin shook his head and smiled before he vanished.

Button whirled around to Brob, "You know him?"

"Many years. Moabitess called him Ayin," replied Brob.

"Wait a minute. You really are seeing someone?" Hazel responded.

"Yes," Button pursued Brob as he pulled maps out of crocks, "Who is he?"

Hazel attempted to talk it through. "Ayin: Hebrew word for eye, to see, the divine light."

"Providence," Button muttered.

Ayin appeared beside Hazel and spoke, "The orphans need you. You must go."

Hazel shivered.

Button approached Hazel after her great revelation. "You just had a sudden urge to return to the orphanage."

"I know this," Hazel gasped. "Why does this surprise me?"

"Ayin spoke. We evacuate caves," Brob explained.

"Caves? Plural?" Button said with a sense of panic.

Brob sorted through the maps looking for something. "Man, on beach, John Mean, a descendant, he has family book."

"I didn't bring the book. I should go back. Wait. There's another book?"

In Brob's haste, he tried to explain. "No. No time. Your book, Moabitess's book. His book, pagan book. My family. He wants me. Wait. No, no, no." He pitched a map to Hazel and pulled Button aside to whisper, "He wants you. To travel. You stay here... I protect you."

Trying to interpret the map, Hazel asked, "What is this?"

"Evacuation plans."

Brob rolled the map and shoved it into a small cylinder and handed it to Hazel.

Hazel grabbed Button. "You must come back with me."

Ayin whispered "No" into Hazel's ears.

"Through the water? No....no." Button walked away from Hazel's hold.

"Caves exit other side of island. In maps, in there. Can get boats and meet us? We pack everything." Brob pointed to the cylinder holding the maps.

Quite baffled and confused, Hazel threw her hands up. "I don't know." She hooked the cylinder to her wetsuit.

When Button mumbled, "Let Providence meet you," Ayin emitted a compassionate smile. He knew what Button would be up against.

* * *

CHEF TIED his round pancake griddle to his waist as the light of day crept into the living room. Hue had several scarves laid out and she meticulously tied them to her outfit. Cowboy attempted to sharpen his spurs with a knife sharpener when Pirate entered in full costume with his sword, one-shot and a compass. Prank, in the corner of the room, checked his full-length prank jacket one more time: shrink wrap, broomstick match-gun, a zip-locked bag with matches, small fire extinguisher and a bicycle horn. Unbeknownst to Prank, they were all curiously watching him, except Hue. As if Hue had a premonition, she quietly approached the window.

"There's a man running," Hue whispered.

All turned in disbelief.

"No one comes here." Prank flatly stated, even though this was the second time it happened. "Cowboy, get Sheba."

* * *

AT THE CAVE, Brob pulled a metal lever, and an elaborate transportation system tracked on chains and rails lowered a metal hinged canister from the ceiling.

"Whoa." Button stood impressed, not just at its structure but at its Byzantine design and its incomprehensible existence.

Seeing her stunned reaction, Brob explained, "Father could forge anything."

"Would love to have met them," Button said under her breath.

Brob took a brief serious pause to respond. "He would use you for bait testing his new weapons. If you didn't die violently, he would go back to redesign it, so you would."

Button stood stunned.

"We will pack the artifacts, and the tracks will take them to the other side of the island," Brob said, continuing his haste as if the power of his words had no effect.

"Wait, wait, WAIT," said Button. "You spoke in complete sentences."

"It comes, it goes," shrugged Brob.

Exasperated, Button slumped to the ground and rested her head on her knees.

Noticing, Brob approached her and asked, "Where you go?"

"To get my father."

"Ayin said you not go back. He never wrong."

Button wavered in indecision.

* * *

THERE WERE THREE SHIPS. John Mean's black double-decker streamlined yacht hung on the water hardly invisible. Its design emanated malice.

Anyone with spiritual eyes could see the trail of aberrations trying to align themselves with this worthless man as he sailed the sea. The second ship, a lower level fishing cruiser, drifted obviously disguised for military use; a large radar unit turned on its bow. The smaller size of the third suggested transportation of men as its main purpose.

Deep in the lower deck of Mean's yacht, Mean snatched a wetsuit from among several in a storage closet. He strutted down the dim hall, then up a couple levels, where he ran into Nahari.

"Have the men suit up and get over here." Mean commanded.

"Yes, sir," remained the only response the yes-man Nahari could give. Nahari had trouble with directions; his mind went a thousand ways to execute any order, and it always had him shifting back and forth. It unnerved Mean.

"Empty out the armory. Make sure each man is fully armed."

"Yes, sir."

Mean resumed his lengthy stride to his dim ominous library. Rushing in and pitching the suit onto his ornate desk, he heard Mother shift in the chair with her head covered.

Mother would normally be free of her predicament by now, but she lacked practice. She struggled with her raging frustrated anger for it distracted her from any opportunity to free herself.

"It's time we got on with it." Mean announced.

He untied her hands and took off her head covering. She squinted and rubbed her wrists, her face so thwarted you could envision the fire about to spew.

When Mean removed her gag, he commanded, "Put on the suit."

"For what reason?"

"Come, come, Mrs. Willow. Blue holes, underground caverns, it's his preferred environment. Did you know your daughter was here?"

Mother bolted from the chair only to be forcefully shoved back. His audacity caused her to rise instantly and slug him right in his solar plexus.

"Ah."

"You lie." Mother said.

As Mean doubled over, she quickly tried to untie her feet.

Mother attempted a third time to best Mean, but she lacked timing. He had seized her by the hair, and his simultaneous quick-draw from behind his belt had her face-to-face with his derringer. He flung her back to the chair.

"This is the last opportunity for you to put a suit on in private."

Mother raised an eyebrow and ceased her struggling.

* * *

SHEBA MOVED from the security system to open the door. Prank shifted uncomfortably at the window, surveying the approaching man through his binoculars.

"You're sure he's okay, Sheba?"

Sheba nodded as she opened the door.

Father burst in. "Sheba, where's Button?"

She shook her head and shrugged.

Father hastily looked from one orphan to the next, hoping to see Button.

Prank announced, "I think they're gonna dive."

But Father kept scanning the children. Sheba intervened by signing their names. "Hue, Pirate, Cowboy, Chef, and Prank at the window. Wait. She's here. What's going on?"

Pirate stepped bravely forward in his costumed array and proclaimed, "We're going to find her. Ms. Hazel, too!"

"What?"

Cowboy offered his best. "Ms. Hazel's diving equipment is missing."

Father whipped around toward Prank at the window, "Who's going to dive? Do they have them?"

Father nudged Prank for the binoculars. "Can I have a look?"

"No," Prank said.

Sheba marched over, snatched Cowboy's hat and whacked

Prank hard with it, then nodded for him to hand the binoculars over.

Father focused the binoculars. He saw commandos in wetsuits aligning the deck on the first boat. "What's your plan?" Father asked Prank.

Fish jumped forward. "We take the boats with this," as he held out a pamphlet.

Father touched it to absorb its contents, *Military Signals for Silent Approach*, then resumed with the binoculars.

"So, what is your plan?" Father reiterated.

"Blimey! Hue, go get the mini-balloons," shouted Pirate.

Hue, shaking her head, walked away from the excitement.

Father stated flatly, "You're going to float over there on balloons."

"No," Prank explained, "They're used for interrogation."

"What?" Father lowered the binoculars.

Pulling on his nostrils, Pirate demonstrated the best he could. "You put them in their nose and blow them up. They'll squeal like pigs on a spit. They'll keep nothing from you."

"You ever hear the phrase 'don't do this at home'?" Father resumed his surveillance. Immediately, he stiffened. There Mother stood in a wetsuit standing on the upper deck of the black yacht surrounded by commandos. They were fitting her with a tank.

Father gasped. "Get the balloons, Hue."

BROB STAYED REVERENT, arms out and eyes closed, as he stood before the first artifact: Goliath's sword, set perfectly within the carved cave wall.

Impatient, Button stated, "I think we should hurry," as she nervously bounced about.

"Shush. I am," Brob responded. His arms came closer to the sword, and it jiggled a bit. A translucent image of Ayin whipped between them and the sword gently lighted in Brob's arms.

He hustled it immediately to the awaiting opened metal container that had dropped down from the tracking system.

"Do you have to do that with all of them?" Button asked.

"No, get armor there," Brob said.

Trotting over to a fancily displayed armor, she realized, "This is a woman's armor." Button took in the sight: the tough woven riding skirt, the metal vested woman's armor, and the glorious small-handled sword. But she quickly reverted to being task oriented rather than intuitive; she hastily grabbed the skirt by the metal clasp.

* * *

IMMEDIATELY, Button stood before King Charles in a dim palatial castle. The Holy Wind had taken her there, yet she still felt like she lingered within her imaginative historical prowess. At this point, Button did not understand she could be sent through time and relive a moment in history, never to change it, mind you, but only to learn from it.

A wigged judge paced before her, choosing his words wisely. "Joan of Arc, are you in the grace of God?"

Button boldly responded, "If I'm not, may God put me there; and if I am, may God so keep me."

* * *

THE SKIRT DROPPED from Button's hand.

"Careful," Brob said.

Button delicately collected the armor and the skirt and slowly walked it over to Brob.

"Joan of Arc ... she burned."

* * *

IN THE WATER under the pier, the orphan team and Father swam toward the smallest boat. Prank held above water the box of matches in a baggy. Cowboy held his cowboy boots up. Fish fiddled with his swimming cap, tucking in the last piece of hair. Fortunately, the morning's sun's rays hid them from sight.

* * *

ON THE TOP deck of Mean's yacht, Mean leaned over the edge to command the suited men waiting on the small boat's diving platform. He pressed his headset, "Team 1, you're up. Inform me when you find any cave. Don't touch anything, understood? Absolutely nothing before I see it. And I want the giant alive." He turned squarely to Mother and flatly spewed, "You will tell me how to safely remove the artifacts."

Studying his face sternly, Mother retorted, "What are you after?"

Mean hesitated, and then slyly said, "I will rule the world."

"That's all? The heavens scoff at you."

"The heavens?" Mean chuckled, "I am of the giant's lineage. Once I acquire the stones, one touch from him, and I will inherit his power. I will ride the Holy Wind."

"You are a fool. Holiness will have nothing to do with evil."

Mean grabbed Mother harshly and pressed his headset. "Deploy. Don't touch ANYTHING."

One by one, five commandos flipped back into the sea from the third boat.

* * *

DRENCHED, Father and his orphan team managed to board the third boat. They divided; each half of the team stood ready on each side of the galley entrance. Father managed a quick peek inside the galley to see what they were up against.

He signaled to all by holding up five fingers. With well-thought perfection, Father militarily signaled Cowboy toward the empty top deck above the entrance. He re-checked the galley. Five commandos checked weaponry that laid on a table.

Father gestured Prank to go over to the other side of the galley entrance opposite him. As he passed, he snatched Prank's shrink wrap and handed it to Hue behind him. Father nodded to Prank.

Prank removed a strike-anywhere-match from his waterproof baggy and attached it to his broomstick rifle. A little lick on his thumb and a touch on his sight and Phft! One match shot to the galley, another to a wastebasket, and another to a basket of towels.

Father signaled to Pirate to cross over and take his place. Then to Prank, Father (really getting into his role) performed a ballet of elaborate signals. Not understanding, Prank just shrugged.

Father simplified a signal for him to pass the other end of the broomstick to Pirate.

No response.

In his frustration, Father got up, grabbed the broomstick, and laid it out for them to hold it firmly down before the entrance.

Smoke drifted from the galley. Commandos slapped and stomped on the fire; however, the smoke overwhelmed them. One started the extinguisher, but the aerosol overwhelmed them as well. Father's plan inevitably worked; the commandos would exit through the door they guarded, and then they'd have them. Up went the broomstick, down went two overloaded commandos. Weapons took to flight; I helped so they wouldn't have access to them, so, they appeared to have their own propulsion. Father snatched the fire extinguisher that flew when the one lost his grip. With lightning speed, he knocked both out with it before they hit the deck.

Two more managed through the exit but Cowboy leaped upon them both and spurred them into submission.

"Ride 'em, Cowboy," Prank squealed in delight.

Chef walloped one with his iron cast skillet and separated him from Cowboy's ride. The other bucked Cowboy off and made his way to the edge.

"Your rope, Cowboy," Fish insisted. The commando hurled himself over the edge as Cowboy tossed his lasso to Fish. Fish tucked a loose string of his hair into his swim cap along the way and expertly, almost inhumanly, dove into the water.

Father could only yell "No" toward Fish but couldn't assist him, for the last commando exited into the waiting translucent shrink wrap he and Hue had strung across the entrance. With perfection, they mummified him from shoulder to toes. He fell over where Hue awaited with a lovely chartreuse scarf, which she hurriedly stuffed into his mouth. The commando mumbled and struggled loudly. Hue held up the shrink wrap.

"I can use more of this. Please be quiet."

The commando lay still, not a syllable uttered.

Father hung over the edge of the boat and searched for Fish. He then scanned the other boats.

"Get down."

All the orphans huddled under the boat's edge. Father flashed one more peek over the edge.

"This is an eternity. I'm going in," he stated.

Prank held Father back. "Fish can stay under for five minutes."

"That's impossible." Father peeked over again, but as he did, Prank elaborately signaled Hue (his inaccuracy evident). Hue tied scarves together and secured one end to the boat's side rope tow.

"It's true, Mr. Willow. It always put Miss Hazel on edge, but he never came close to drowning. Give him some time," Cowboy said, attempting to give Hue some time to finish her mission.

Prank peeked over. "Wait, they're looking this way." All of them ducked except Prank. Hue took his cue and tied the other end of the scarf line to Father's ankle.

Father peeked again. "All clear, I'm going in." He slipped over the side only to find himself upside down with his head dangling above the water level.

A face surfaced on the water in front of him. He gasped then gaped, "Hazel?"

"Willow?" Hazel removed her mouthpiece.

Fish popped up as well.

"Where have you been?" Father asked.

A fully lassoed commando surfaced. He spat out Hazel's portable mouthpiece and shouted, "Help, get me out of—"

Upside down and frustrated, Father punched the man out.

"And from such a refined position. Well done, Willow," said Hazel.

Never being able to best Hazel, Father, puffed up a bit, smiled, acknowledging the compliment.

Hazel whispered, "Cut him down, Pirate."

Father plummeted into the ocean.

* * *

MEAN STILL HELD Mother close to him. He leaned over the bow side of the top deck of his yacht and pressed his radio. "Team Two, head out."

Ten commandos jumped one-by-one off the yacht's stern diving platform.

"Time to go, Mrs. Willow. We're next."

* * *

IN FRONT of the yacht's bow, Hazel, Father, and the orphans dog-paddled through the water.

"Try again, Cowboy," Hazel encouraged.

Cowboy threw his lasso once again to grasp a tow hook.

Hazel faced Father and asked, "Are you sure?"

"It was Mother." To Cowboy, "Try again."

This time he looped it.

"Careful, slowly, slowly," Father said as Cowboy pulled the loop tightly over the hook.

Hazel noted Father's countenance, "You're concerned."

"This is beyond concern, Hazel."

"Willow, my sister is the greatest juggler. She can work herself out of—"

"This time she got caught." Father tugged the rope and began his climb. "Don't come up until I tell you."

As Father climbed, Hazel took off her tank, clipped her harpoon to her back, and fidgeted with some other gadgets. Father gazed back, "I see you've faithfully laid aside your gadgets. Where did you get them?"

"Same place I got this?" Hazel held up a gun-type weapon.

Straining in his climb a bit, Father said, "I don't recognize its make. I've read every book and design."

Hazel began her climb, "Then you ought to know I designed it myself."

Prank put Hue on his back to prepare to climb.

"Whatever for?" said Father.

Prank began his climb, with Hue in tow and Chef waiting in the wings. Meanwhile, Fish just enjoyed swimming around in circles.

"For times like this," Hazel said.

Father stopped right before the edge and muttered, "The gadget queen. When are you girls going to give this up?" Father heaved himself over the top of the boat.

* * *

FATHER, with Hazel and some orphans, approached the low diving area on both sides from a level above. Hazel lifted a bucket of dirty water in passing. John Mean and Mother stood on the edge of the platform ready to dive with two commandos. Two more stood before the ladder leading down to the platform on Hazel and Father's level.

"You four will stay by me at all times. Let the others take the point," said Mean.

Father and Hazel peeked around from opposite sides.

"When we're under, keep an eye on this one," Mean instructed.

Mother exerted herself one more time to gain her freedom, but the commandos would have nothing of it.

Enraged, Father sprang into action; he grabbed Prank's broomstick, caught the two commandos at the top of the stairs by surprise and whacked them into the water.

"Treasure," Mother yelled.

Mean jabbed his pistol in Mother's rib and said, "Let's go."

Father leaped onto the platform as Mean muscled Mother into the water.

The two remaining commandos pointed their weapons at Father as Mother submerged by the force of her escorts.

Hazel gasped at all of this and mumbled, "Blast it, Willow. You couldn't wait." She scanned for the commandos' positions again, coded her electronic underwater Taser, and clipped a power pack onto it. "In thirty seconds, make some noise," she instructed Hue, Fish, and Chef.

Hazel stepped from her hiding spot and shot twice. Two Taser projectiles hit the two commandos.

The two doubled over to try to avoid the shot; Father immediately dove into the water in search of Mother. Their thirty seconds up, the Orphans began screaming, the only diversion they could think of. Prank and Cowboy charged from the other side with a rebel call and leaped onto the diving deck.

"Don't touch them," Hazel yelled.

One commando tried to remove his projectile and the other shot toward where Father dove. Hazel hurled the bucket of dirty water on one commando, and he immediately convulsed.

"Prank." Hazel launched the bucket to him. Taking the cue, he dipped it in the water and chucked the water at the other commando. His spasmodic contortions brought him to the ground immediately.

Hazel leaped down onto the deck, put on special gloves she had tucked in her suit and grabbed the men's weapons. She punched a button on her projectile gun, and the commando's spasms ceased. However, she kept one of their rifles pointed toward them both.

When the orphans saw her holding them at gunpoint, they simultaneously gaped. This was the second time they saw her do this.

Both commandos lurched forward to grab Hazel.

POP. POP. Her shots landed just shy of their feet. Obediently, they backed off.

"Whoa," the orphans said in unison.

"Tie them up, Cowboy."

Father surfaced. "They're gone. I can't find them." He collapsed on the wave-beaten deck, spent.

"I know where they're going, Willow," Hazel said as she unhooked the cylinder of Brob's maps. "It's in here."

Hope filled Father's eyes as Hazel tossed it to him. He opened it, smiled, and managed to say, "Let's take this boat."

* * *

FIVE ALREADY-PACKED CANISTERS hung from the ceiling's tracking system. Brob and Button snatched all the cylindered maps from the crocks and rushed them to the last canister. Brob rushed back.

"But I got the last one," Button yelled.

"No, one missing, small one," Brob called back as he checked another crock.

"What about the Machine of the Wise Ones?" Button asked as she stood before it curiously.

"Leave. We come back. Machine hard to move. Too much time. Here." Brob held up a flat rock with map etchings on it.

"What is it?"

With a sheepish smile, Brob answered, "Map to rum cave."

Button sternly approached Brob.

"Make tourist attraction?" he said to justify his task.

Button wagged her finger at Brob when a smoke bomb landed

on the cave floor. With agility that Button had not seen previously from Brob, he threw it back into the water.

Backing up to the cave's rear wall, Button whispered, "Someone's coming."

Brob swiftly secured the last container when another smoke bomb rattled toward him. Smartly, he covered it with a crock. PUFF. It went off.

"Pull the lever. Now!" Brob called out.

Button's fear had backed her right into the lever mechanism. She threw her whole weight on the lever and couldn't get it down.

"It's stuck!"

BOOM. A smoke bomb exploded in mid-air. Brob scooped Button and pulled the lever with choreographed ease. As a loud CLANK echoed, the canisters made their way up the tracking system then trailed parallel to the ceiling. They disappeared into the high tunnel to their pre-planned destination.

"We go."

The smoke grew thicker. With Button in hand, Brob hustled for the dim portion of the cave. They fled down a lengthy shadowy tunnel.

* * *

THE FIVE POINT COMMANDOS took a defensive stance over the cave's ledge. As the smoke lifted, the one in charge signaled a search. One very frightened commando made the mistake of hugging the cave's wall. He bumped the cross and plumb line, The Machine of the Wise Ones. Taking a step forward, he froze for a moment, eyes searching and then the commando jumped 180 degrees. Nothing appeared in his vision, as if he had any visual acuity at all with the military garb he had on. He didn't realize the Machine had rotated off the wall and began to measure him from behind.

As the smoke dissipated, five more commandos came over the ledge to see this scared one's dilemma.

Catching his team's approaching concern, he said, "What?"

Then he peered behind and startled. The Machine reacted with precision and began again revolving around him, measuring. Another from his team batted at it.

Doubling its speed, The Machine herded the two together and started to measure them both in all ways imaginable. The three from his team and the five additional arrivals pulled back to the ledge.

John Mean and his two escorts come over the ledge dragging Mother out of the water.

To the five, he commanded, "Guard her." Mean's escorts pulled Mother to her feet and began unsnapping her tank.

When Mean took his off, he eyed the predicament the two had gotten into. "I told you not to touch anything." He turned to Mother. "Stop it."

"It only stops when it is finished."

"Finishing what?"

Mother sighed heavily because of his ignorance. "Measuring every possible measurement. The more movement and people added the longer it'll take."

"How long?" Mean asked, but Mother just smiled and stood in silence. Mean signaled the five; they pressed into Mother with their knives pulled.

"Provided they stand still, three days. Three weeks if they move again." Mother's smile remained even as the peril escalated about her.

"We're moving. Find the exit. Keep a wide berth," Mean ordered as the five followed him. His two bodyguards pushed Mother forward.

The scared captured commando could only manage a peep, "What shall we do, sir?" The Machine whirled at an incredible speed around the two. Mean and the rest of his crew walked past them.

"Sir?"

They disappeared through the back tunnel.

* * *

BUTTON AND BROB had entered a hundred-foot diameter circular cave where a massive stone forge stood in the center. Ancient weapons, meteor hammers, holy water sprinklers, tridents, flails, and other items hung on the walls.

"My," was all Button could manage to speak. Brob turned on the lights.

"Family trade," Brob explained.

"You made all of these?"

"Over years."

Button meandered curiously, with Brob watching her every step. The holy water sprinkler attracted her. "They don't all look dangerous," Button said.

As she stepped toward a raised portion of the floor, Brob swiftly scooped Button up and said, "All deadly. You stand by me." He set her down.

Brob pulled a heavy metal lever. A long, narrow canister with a serpent's head carved on it chained down from the ceiling. Brob picked his way carefully, guiding Button's steps to the holding place of the staff with the fiery serpent atop.

"Is that what I think it is?" Button asked.

Once again, in full reverence, Brob held out his arms in a calm prayer. Again, with a slight appearance of Ayin, the staff plopped into his arms.

"Many Israelites bitten. Spoke against Almighty. Servant made serpent to save."

Brob reverently started to pack it.

Button looked up and saw no canisters, "Why only pack the one item? What about all the rest?"

They could hear feet shuffling and the faint barking of orders from the tunnel entrance.

Button panicked. "Brob, close it up. Maybe I can get us out of here." She reclined her head on his shoulder as he continued to ritually pack. Button squinted as if she could force her ability to travel.

"Have to pack right. Ready lever. Walk straight to it. No, waver." Brob commanded.

Button nervously muttered as the sounds of men approaching grew louder, "Like I could do the last one."

Brob raised his hand like the end of a rodeo cattle tie. "Done," he called.

Surprisingly, Button eased the lever down with no trouble at all. As the canister tracked upward, Brob scooped Button and zigzagged a specific path toward the opposite tunnel.

CHAPTER 13

EVACUATING THE ARTIFACTS

FATHER LED HAZEL AND THE orphans down the stairs of Mean's yacht to the narrow hallway. Prank held a bucket of water in hopes he could throw it on someone the next time. He stood expectant - all wrapped up in the adventure.

"No, Prank. You watch the children; stay here and wait for us to check it out," Father whispered.

When she saw Prank about to open his mouth in protest, Hazel stopped him with a stern look. She held a finger to her mouth, notifying all the children to stay silent. They all sat in obedience.

Father started down the hallway, leaning an ear on every door, each time shaking his head "no." He signaled Hazel to check the ones on the opposite end of the hall.

Hazel pressed her ear against the third door and heard humming. She waved Father over and cracked open the door. All the orphans strained their necks to view their investigation.

Inside, Nahari poured himself a large drink. He patted and ran his hand over the ornate desk with great pride. With a large sigh, he reclined in John Mean's office chair with his feet up. He gulped his drink; his false sense of importance emulated by him. Funny how Earth Dwellers can quickly role play self-importance. Regardless, there wasn't anybody left on the boat.

Hazel closed the door and signaled Father to go beyond to the next door. She handed him the specialized gun, and he whispered, "The bucket?" She grabbed him, "Go. Trust me," she whispered. She signaled "back up" down the hallway to the orphans.

With a shrug, Father proceeded to the next door. When he arrived, Hazel rushed Nahari and threw his drink on him.

Splat. Nahari tumbled over in his chair. Scrambling up, he grabbed a gun from the desk drawer and yelled, "What was that for?"

He vainly brushed his shirt off, but Hazel strategically moved to draw his peripheral vision from Father, who approached from the rear door.

"Stop. Why are you here?" Nahari blurted.

"I don't know. Why are you here?" Hazel asked.

Nahari pressed forward slyly, smiling, "To guard the boat. And I think I'm doing a very good job of it."

"Really?" Father said behind him as he zapped him on the wet spot of his shirt with Hazel's specialized pistol.

Whirling around, Nahari contorted to the ground.

Hazel yelled, "Come on in, children."

Scurrying a bit too soon through the doorway, Hazel realized they had been outside listening. Puppy-eyed and ready as they were, she couldn't chastise them. "All right, subdue this man. But first, use these gloves to take out those prods."

While Father and Hazel searched the library, the children roped Nahari to a chair, shrink wrapped his body, stuffed his mouth with scarves, hung a cast iron frying pan on his head, shot a few rubber bands to keep his head up and put some spurs in his ears.

"Willow, over here," said Hazel.

"Of course, he has a safe. Can you blow it?" Father asked.

In a matter of seconds, Hazel readied herself to blast.

"To the back wall children and cover your ears." Again, their dumbfounded expression made her shush them to the wall. When Prank wouldn't budge, she simply said, "Your choice, son."

Father appealed, "Do what she asks, Prank." But Hazel would have no discussion on the matter. KA-BOOM. The locking mechanism popped off the safe. Prank jolted back, no clue as to what had just occurred.

Father patted him on the back, "Sometimes blind obedience is a necessity in life."

Hazel and Father surveyed the contents of the safe, finding Mean's own leather book.

"She told me about the one in Ma'mah's attic. I had no idea there were two," said Hazel.

"Did Mother?" Father asked.

"She said nothing about it. You'd better take a good look at this, Willow. You have the specialty."

"This Mean, does he have any specialties? He's obviously more than what Mother bargained for," asked Father.

Hazel turned her head away from Father and shook her head slowly. "I haven't a clue. We need to navigate quickly to the other side of the island."

"For the artifacts? My family is at stake."

Hazel's shocked disappointment almost turned to tears.

Father regretted his outburst. The orphans stood with their heads down.

Unhooking the small cylinder from her suit and opening it, Hazel said, "The Keeper made a pre-planned evacuation. I assure you, Willow, the family is my priority. This is where he took Sister. Button and the Keeper are there." She handed him the two maps. "You know I have no navigational skills. Perhaps you can wrap your specialty around these."

Father quickly laid the maps out on a work table and studied both acutely. "By this, perhaps there is a way to save both," he muttered.

Hazel smiled.

"Pirate, time to sail. Do you think you can manage the second boat?"

"Aye, Sir," Pirate responded.

Father wisped his hand over the evacuation map. "Our resident Giant is wise. Such an elaborate system of subterfuge. FISH."

"Aye, Sir."

"Time to swim," Father quickly turned to Hazel. "Can you rig some type of tow snaps underneath this yacht with Fish's help?"

"Can do," Hazel responded as she slipped the leather-bound book toward Father. "Take some time with this, we'll manage up top. Children! Stop taunting the poor man. Up with you."

The children scurried out.

"It won't open, you know," Father forlornly explained.

"Huh?" Hazel turned a page.

Father flipped another page and another. "Ours only paged when it wanted to."

Hazel thought for a moment. "Evil is easily revealed in the presence of holiness." She pats Father on the shoulder. "I have full confidence in you, Willow."

Father finally recognized Hazel's new convictions. It occurred as an endearing moment for him. "Indeed, you have changed, Hazel. I'll try to commit it to memory."

"Try? I thought you had the gift?"

He brushed the book. "It's odd. It seems like it has some type of dampening mechanism. Let me work on it."

* * *

ENTERING THE SECOND CAVE, Mean's entourage assessed from the entrance.

"Clear," the frontman said.

Mother and Mean entered with his two bodyguards.

Awestruck and bright-eyed, Mean blurted, "This is fabulous. Such weaponry. The quality is amazing." He looked back to

Mother, who stood with her sly smile. "Let's not be hasty, men," he ordered. "You four fan out slowly."

Mean faced off with Mother. "What? You know something."

The commandos were almost to the center of the room.

"Seems clear, sir," one said.

Another stood about two steps from a rock.

"Keep going," Mean ordered.

The rock crushed when a commando stepped on it. They all had a moment of stillness before they heard CLICK CLICK.

With sheer speed, a meteor hammer with two spherical spines (on opposite ends) released from the cave's wall. It circled the militant powerfully.

"Back up. Slowly, the same way you went in," Mean instructed.

As they got closer to the cave's entrance tunnel once again, the meteor hammer whipped toward the commando who stepped on the rock and WACK. CLUNK. Down went the man.

Mean yelled, "Freeze. Don't move," as he pushed Mother to the entrance wall. "What's the trigger?"

Mother struggled with all her might and almost broke free when the two bodyguards slammed her into the wall, hitting her head hard.

"Tell me." Mean said.

Mother mumbled through her cloudy head, "Just watch."

When Mean whipped back around toward his men, the downed commando had an autonomic leg jerk; his foot hit a rock. CLICK CLACK.

"The damage is already done," Mother said.

The commando in the middle of the cave whipped around and stepped on another rock. CLICK CLACK.

"It's the rocks. Don't step on them." Mean held back his body-guards, bracing for the next two weapons.

A wide-pronged trident routed up a track and hurled toward the commando who had tripped on a rock, pinning him to the stone floor. He made the unfortunate mistake of grabbing another rock to try to pull through the prongs.

CLICK CLACK.

The commando, in perfect panic mode, thrashed another rock. An ornate nunchaku released toward the downed commando.

"Don't move," Mean commanded. The commando froze.

The nunchaku hovered a moment, then knocked him out.

"Bad advice," said Mother.

Mean said to his two assigned commandos, "We can't walk to the exit. We'll make our way after these next weapons are released."

A holy water sprinkler on a club catapulted to the trident-trapped raider and lingered above his head.

The commando screamed, "Forgive me."

The sprinkler's spikes punched out. Unable to control himself, the raider screamed. The sprinkler launched toward the entrance, Mean in his path.

"Now." Mean lifted Mother, shot a grappling hook to the ceiling and pushed off to swing toward the opposite exit.

The sprinkler met its destination, a large rock that clung to the wall. CLICK CLACK, CLICK CLACK. Every weapon released. The two bodyguards immediately shot their hooks to the ceiling and pushed off. The remaining three standing in the middle of the cave attempted to pick their paths carefully to the exit, but they were flung, chucked and heaved to the ground.

Mean managed to escape the free-for-all but didn't consider the extra weight of Mother when he landed. They both lost their balance and fell backward. One bodyguard swept in and managed to nab Mother away safely, leaving Mean struggling for balance.

The second bodyguard swooped in alongside Mean and landed securely. His kneejerk reaction to latch on to Mean's bullet vest and jerk him to the exit didn't succeed because he didn't consider the physics of the matter. He pulled Mean to safety but catapulted himself within the cave on a rock. CLICK CLACK. A huge shining metal shield, with blinding force, came straight down and pounded him two inches into the rock floor.

Infuriated, Mean seized Mother and pointed to his remaining

guard. "Lead the way," he spewed. "You will tell me every trick the giant has up his sleeve before we meet it, or I will kill you. I want those stones. All of them."

Mother, having none of it, pressed closer to Mean. In her righteous anger, she said, "I have a leather-bound book, John Mean. The book gives me the answers you're looking for. You think those stones will give you the power you're after? You don't even have the knowledge, the revelation, or the power of the true book of life. How is it that you think your book will supersedes mine?"

With super-human strength, Mean put Mother in a choke hold and lifted her up the cavern wall. "I too, have a leather-bound book." Mother's eyes widened in disbelief. "And this world will serve me."

Mother's squashed vocal cords barely managed. "You are a puppet being used by evil. I am no help to you." Without warning, a wave of a mighty wind blew through the cavern, forcing Mean to release Mother. Both thrashed through the wind down the exit tunnel trying to regain their balance. Mean managed to nab Mother as they went. Mother took the opportunity to take a good look back down the tunnel. There, as Mean held her captive once again, stood the silhouette of Ayin at the exit before the second cave. She squinted to grasp more of her vision; yet as the wind ceased, he disappeared.

* * *

Entering the third cave, Brob immediately pulled a lever. The tracking system continued to move the above containers toward the exit route out of the cave; they did not come down. Button scanned the sparse cave that had no exit. It was a dead end. She regarded the cave's limited contents: a small ratty wooden trunk by the wall, a round stoned water pool in the center of the cave, an axe head, and a crooked stick on the pool's edge.

"Brob? Where's the way out?" Button asked.

Brob rushed into the pool. He held his hand out. "Come quickly."

Button managed a stammered mutter of "Flummoxes," repeatedly.

Brob stood in the pool. "I swim good. Here." Brob leaped out of the pool, went to the lone wooden box, and opened it. He flipped out a loincloth, one from the old Tarzan movies.

"See. John Weissmuller."

"What?"

"Olympic swimmer played Tarzan. Taught him how."

Mean's muffled voice traveled from a corridor. Button backed to the pool. Brob dropped the loincloth and rushed to the entrance. He clobbered the rocks at the entrance of the cave until they tumbled to rubble, blocking it.

Seeing Button back at the pool, Brob rushed back and grabbed the axe head.

"Axe owner thought axe lost." He tossed the axe gently into the pool. "Remember story?"

Button watched in disbelief. "Goodness," she said, and the stick twitched a bit, then zoomed into the water.

"How we go," Brob explained. "see?"

The stick brought the axe up to the surface.

Shuffled rock noises came from the entrance.

"Mean comes," said Brob.

"We could travel," Button said as she grabbed Brob and closed her eyes tightly.

"Rocks explode. No time." Brob snatched Button and stepped into the pool.

"Wait, let me try again." In desperation, she closed her eyes and inhaled a large cleansing breath.

Brob heaved the axe down with great force, then grabbed the stick. The crooked stick led the way. It propelled Brob and Button at a great velocity through a vast underwater tunnel at the bottom of the pool.

* * *

BROB AND BUTTON shot straight into the air far above the receiving pool. Down they plummeted into a great splash. Brob immediately leaned Button over the side of the new pool and began patting her on the back. Button couldn't determine the worse, Brob's forceful pats, or choking the water out of her lungs.

"Okay, little Moabitess?" Brob's countenance spoke volumes of concern. Brob separated the stick from the anvil axe and laid it on the pool's edge. He resumed his pats with both hands.

"No, no, stop," Button managed between gags. "I'll be fine. Go."

Brob leaped out, knowing the importance of time; there were many items to pack in this cavern. As he pulled the lever, several containers tracked down. Brob flipped a light switch.

With Button's waterlogged and blurry vision, the vast cavern and its artifacts slowly came into clear view.

"All right?" Brob asked, still worried about her.

Button slowly nodded, "Uh huh...I need to purchase a swim-suit." Button slithered out of the pool. Experiencing some sea legs, she wobbled backward toward the pool's ledge. Correcting herself, she heard a PLOP.

The axe dropped in the pool.

Trying to correct her error, she flung herself to the pool's edge and grabbed the stick, but it flew out of her hand. Weakly, Button exclaimed, "Nyoo. Uh, Brob, the axe, and stick. Will it come back?"

Brob approached her and scratched his head. "May go other cave. Velocity slow? We hurry." Brob hurried back to the containers and started to load large trunks.

Button took a moment to scan the cave. It had two wide open-ings leading to other caverns. There were many wooden trunks and a strange curtain hanging with a long tear in it, perhaps over another entrance? An odd-looking rock stuck to the stone wall on the opposite side. Close by, two silver trumpets hung on the wall. She reached for them to help but Brob yelled, "No."

Startled, Button jumped back.

"No. Warn when they come. Pack last," Brob explained.

"What do they sound like?"

"Dunno. One blast, leaders come. Two blasts, whole congregation." Brob pulled another lever. "Queen of Sheba gold," he mumbled. He hefted a larger wooden chest and slammed it into the container. Off it went. Clank, clank up the tracking system. He paused and said, "Come. Help Queen of Sheba spices."

Button and Brob rushed over to the area filled with large over-sized crockery. By the time he had two of them loaded, Button still strained to pick up one.

"No, no. There. Small boxes. Precious oils," Brob instructed.

Still waterlogged, she shuffled over. But curiosity got her. She opened a box while Brob worked. Corked vials were aligned in the box. She opened one, and a tiny bit of vapor flew up to her nostrils.

"Wow." She danced around. "I feel great."

Brob rushed over and corked the vial and closed the box. "No play. Very powerful. Very medicinal." He picked up all eight boxes of vials and rushed off. Button footed to the next crate and opened it.

"Nyoo!"

Startling her, Brob solemnly stood behind her. "Represents Kings of ancestors."

Button reached in and struggled to lift one with its weight. "Five golden tumors. Amazing. They still exist?"

Brob snatched it away from her and secured the box.

"What's in this one?" Button pointed at another crate.

"Five golden mice. Offering ancestors made. Returned ark." Brob heaved it into a container and heaved a great sigh.

"Is the ark here?" Button enthusiastically asked.

Brob frowned and shook his head. "No time," he said. "Keeper slow."

"What can I do?"

Brob reverently picked up a long rope with a loop tied at the end and wrapped it around Button's waist and around his arm.

"What's this for?"

"Keep close. Little Moabitess curious."

Brob headed for the other cavern opening, while Button just stood there looking at the loop around her waist as its end lengthened. Then, as she overheard Brob shout, "The prominent woman's bed," she saw a bright peep of light piercing through the covering curtain. Attracted to it, she gently crept to it.

CRASH. SCRAPE. Button startled. Brob's meek voice stammered in the background. "Sorry bed, nice bed,"

Button slipped her hand into her button purse as she returned her attention to the light.

Older Helena appeared behind her saying, "Holy, Holy." Whipping around, Button saw no one; however, she clearly heard the voice of Helena. She turned again to the curtain, and now a strong light coming from behind it enveloped the curtain's gray color.

Brob cleared his throat.

Button whipped around, seeing him standing there. "What is it?"

"Ayin's eyes are uncovered," Brob explained.

"Why?"

"Things happen now."

Brob quickly led Button to the opposite stone wall where the rock jutted from the wall. He wrapped the rope around her, secured it a couple of times and looped the long end to a holding ring on the cave's wall with a tight tie.

Ayin, in all brilliance, whooshed in saying, "They're coming," and out he left.

"I think I have a pair," said Brob as he frantically searched the rock wall. Finding what he wanted, he pushed a specific rock formation. Nothing happened. He whacked it with a punch, leaving a shattered hole in the wall.

"There." He reached in and found a custom-fit pair of sunglasses. He put them on. "Good."

"What's happening?" Button said, in a bit of a panic as the light continued to intensify.

"Principalities and powers will battle. You stay with rope."

"As in Biblical proportions?"

Brob halted; disappointedly, he shook his head. Looking back to Button, he said, "Have you not seen? Have you not heard? Yes."

* * *

THE COMMANDO, Mean and Mother stood before the lone pool. The commando returned from his search, "All clear, sir, but I see no exit."

The axe, balancing on the stick, plopped to the surface by the stick within the pool. The commando shifted to point his weapon at it.

Mother chuckled, "All done here. Now what?"

Mean eyed the stick and axe as it floated toward the edge.

"We'll have to go back," Mother beamed.

Mean picked up the axe and stick, he said, "You forget who I am." He gently let the axe sink and quickly put the stick in above it. It dove and surfaced with the axe. This time, he dropped the axe in; the stick whooshed from his hand after it.

* * *

FATHER FLIPPED pages back and forth, scanning them. He looked very perplexed trying to put things into memory. Hue stood nonchalantly beside him occasionally gazing at the book. He flipped one page, mumbling, "Three artifacts." He flipped another page and mumbled again, "the sling stones...Hue, what did I just say?"

"The sling stones," Hue said.

"No, before that. What did I say before that?"

Hue thought for a moment, "Nothing. You didn't say nothing."

Hazel entered, "I think I've got these, Willow. Where's Fish?" She tried to juggle the tow clips she made but one fell and *Phtt*, it self-inserted to the floor. "Oh, dear," Hazel said.

"We have a problem," Father confessed. "I can't retain anything in this book. The minute I turn the page, it's gone."

"Nyoo!" Hazel said as her sister would have said it.

"Look," Father explained as he turned back the page: "This page speaks of three artifacts, and when I turn it to this one, it talks about the five sling stones of David." He looked at Hazel. "Tell me what the first one said."

Hazel opened her mouth to answer but could only say, "This is your expertise, Willow. You've got to fight this and come up with a way to remember this book. Wait, write it down."

Scrambling for paper and pen, Father scribbled an explanation behind the number "1".

He did the same for the second, but as he wrote, item number "1" disappeared off the page, and no one had a recollection.

"We'll take it with us."

Father shook his head, "And risk Mean getting it? No, it's going out to sea when I'm finished."

Hazel and Father stood dumbfounded and defeated.

Hue whispered, "When I don't want to forget, I tie one of these." She flipped one of her scarves in the air. "I tie it to my body to help me remember."

Father flipped to another page. "My Lord. He commands a spiritual armada."

"What?" asked Hazel.

Hue tied a scarf on Father's arm. "Here, for the arma…armad… what-ya-call-it?"

"Armada," Father said as he flipped the page forward and looked at the scarf on his arm.

Simultaneously, Hazel and Father yelled, "Armada."

Hazel grabbed Hue and kissed her as Father gazed at the next page. "He's after a Traveler, no... someone who travels. He seeks their power."

"Someone who travels?" Hazel said, "Everybody travels."

"It's Button; he's after Button. It's how we came to be here. It's like the wind, a Holy Wind."

"Phillip the Evangelist," whispered Hazel, "Miraculous."

"Exactly," Father responded.

Hue tied a small scarf to Father's button. Father hugged her.

"Hazel, we must hurry."

"You and Hue keep at this. Pirate's leading us as fast as he can. Fish, Fish," Hazel called out, "you have some swimming to do."

* * *

MEAN STOOD near the center of the pool.

"You think I stand here weak, with one man. You will escort me. I know there's an opening in the bottom of this pool which leads to where they went. Just a couple more steps." Mean stepped forward one step and dropped five feet in the pool. He looked at Mother—"You will escort me"—as he climbed out.

"I will not."

Mean picked up the floating axe and stick and set it on the pool's edge.

Mean raised his hands outward, threw his head backward and waved his hands until shadows of darkness appeared. The evil revolved around him until his hands commanded it toward the bottom of the pool. In it went, causing a large whirlpool.

With a large breath, Mean picked up the axe, stood on the pool's edge, and raised it, "Madam, it is time to go. It's a matter of velocity. Velocity will take us to the next cave."

"No," Mother said. "You're wrong."

"Don't you want to see your daughter?" He turned to the commando. "I'll send this back to you."

Mean hurled the axe into the whirlpool with all his might.

Mother lunged for the stick (I might have helped her). SHE GOT IT! It jerked her into flight at an unusually fast pace as it chased the axe. But Mean seized Mother's foot as she flew, piggy-backing on her flight.

* * *

The light intensified.

"Brob…"

Then it burst, blinding Button.

Heavenly Powers and Principalities whooshed over the pool forming a barricade preventing the short, dark, ugly spirits anguishing to enter. Two Heavenly Spirits assisted Brob, accelerating his packing. They appeared as vapor, then as men, transforming back and forth.

Unable to see, Button could only feel their presence.

This is where, I, Samandiriel, received orders to step in. What a freedom to be released into the realm of man for His Glory. Though in her spirit she had suspected I existed, this was the first time Button met me.

"I can't see," Button said as she blindly searched.

I, Samandiriel, Angel of Imagination, hovered over her. "Don't be afraid, mighty warrior. I will help you see."

Frozen in her experience (the spiritual has that effect on humans), Button's eyes slowly adjusted to the hustling amazement.

"Ayin, the eye of God, has summoned Seraphim to protect the Holy items. It is the reason for the great light. You'll not see him, but I can assist…to filter the intensity for you." Powers zoomed, whooshed and soared over the pool. Initially, they resembled the haze around Button's imaginative state, but they soon took the shape of an impenetrable mist. The Principalities of God (who decide who will be rulers of the earth) knew Mean's intent to rule the earth, so they were also present. Their magnificent color always pleased me.

To the human eye, they appeared as light rays, but for us of course, they resembled the human form of guardian angels. They stood ready behind the misty barrier the Power's created.

The nasty spirits' entry intensified and pushed the barrier. They took the form of tormenting faces that were being stampeded by cattle—their sole motivation to push forward.

"They're getting bigger," Button whispered.

"Yes." I quietly responded.

"Brob? He's all right?" Button turned to see a robust spirit heave the ivory throne of Solomon to Brob. Brob, in turn, tossed it into a molded container and slammed the door closed. The container tracked upward.

"The Keeper is well," I explained, but the dark spirits were advancing before I could make her understand.

"They're coming for me," Button realized.

"Yes. Cling to the One who holds you, Button. Think only on his Name." With that, I wheeled off to join the battle.

The rope, having a plan of its own, began to pull Button back to the wall. It knew what approached.

"Hold on," Brob called out. "Almost there."

The dark spirits began a new tactic; they were more annoying than threatening to us, but for Button's education, we allowed them to display their fear-inducing habit. All the evil spirits combined into one horrific massive figure resembling their master, the one tossed down ages ago. The heavenlies allowed it to advance at my nod.

The evil monstrosity pushed the barrier's limit, but the Holy Rope of the temple pulled Button back with each advancement until she pressed against the wall. Button screamed and threw her arms out, trying desperately for a chance to travel. That's when I intervened. Still holding sentry behind the Powers' mist, the Heavenly Principalities went from their lighted form to their guardian human form and I, Samandiriel, joined them with one big push. "Enough," I said.

Button stood in disbelief with her hands outstretched, one about to hit the unusual large rock jutting from the wall. The intense light, the spiritual battle, had ceased.

In a flash, Brob zoomed over and grabbed her hand before it hit the jutted rock.

"Rock of Horeb. No touch. Very bad, especially for you."

Button gave him a curious expression; I think the children of God interpret this face as the vocal idiom "really?"

"I untie." In haste, Brob untied the Holy Temple Rope from the iron ring, and it instantly slapped him across the face. Button gasped, still wrapped in the rope's hold.

"What just happened?"

"Got slapped by Holy Rope."

"No, before." The Holy Rope tightened on Button's midriff. She inhaled swiftly.

"Rope Holy. Respect rope. Rope knows you know. To ask, you deny." Brob reverently bent down to gather the end of the rope. "Nice rope," he said.

Button stood annoyed. The rope tightened. Button gasped.

As Brob picked up the end of the rope, he patted and wrapped it lovingly and came to where it held Button. "You gonna let her go? Nice rope." It tightened on Button again making her breathless.

Brob leaned into Button, "You confess. Rope won't let go."

Button gasped out, "In His sovereignty, I saw the army of the Lord protecting us, His chosen, and someone named Sam." The rope loosened and dropped to the ground. Button stepped out, and Brob wrapped it up quickly.

"Sam? Moabitess loved Sam. Spiritual Sam," Brob noted Button's state of shock.

He leaned face to face and smiled kindly. "Spiritual can be fun, dangerous, satisfying or terrifying." Brob stroked her cheek. "You'll see more. Keep an eye open for it." He paused and patted her on her head.

"Come, we go," Brob said as he closed the rope in its special container and sent it on its way.

Button traced the container as it rose to the massive height of the cave. She saw below the tracking containers a short ladder very high up.

"Our way out?" she asked.

"Uh, huh," said Brob. "We climb cave wall to ladder."

Just then, the silver trumpets blew two muffled blasts within their container. "They're coming." Button said.

CHAPTER 14

MEAN'S COMMANDOS

THE STICK MOTHER CLUNG TO had already attached itself to the axe head. When she was about to breach the new cave's pool surface, the stick launched her further above the cool water.

Mean, still clasped onto Mother's foot, flew about fifteen feet beyond Mother, for he couldn't hold on any longer. The propulsion sent him farther, causing him to land hard on the floor, but Mother landed in the pool next to the axe which had separated from the stick. She quickly released the stick to avoid taking another venture through the tunnel connecting the two caves. The stick headed after the axe.

Brob charged Mean.

"Ah, Ah." Mean had instantly rolled out of his landing and had Mother at knifepoint dragging her out of the pool. "Up and out, now." Mean pulled on Mother mercilessly as Brob backed off. Mean searched around the cave.

"Force not here. Met stronger force," Brob said.

"I'm so out of practice," Mother whispered, as she crawled out of the pool. She tried to see through her water-logged eyes.

Button rushed forward, "Mother. Mother, you're alive." But Brob held her back.

"Button, darling. I'm sorry you're here," Mother moaned.

"No, no, I think I'm exactly where I'm supposed to be," answered Button.

If I were an Earth Dweller, I would have performed a choreographed cheer. The epiphany of Button's destiny began to penetrate her fearful mind.

Mother managed a grim smile.

Mean gathered Mother behind his knife and dragged her toward Brob.

Brob rushed him. The knife scraped Mother's skin.

"No," Button screamed.

"Let's clear things up, shall we?" Mean began.

"Don't do it. Whatever he says, don't do it," Mother said.

Mother's words only made Mean tighten his grip.

"Where are the sling stones?" Mean asked.

Looks of determination and uncertainty flipped between Mother, Button, and Brob. Their intentional silence would not do for the overruling Mean.

"Okay, I'll start. I have two. How many do you have?"

Button started to open her mouth, but Mother shook her head.

"Do you think I care about this woman?" Mean said as he dragged her closer to them, shifting the knife precariously.

Button screamed. Mother yelped.

"I have two." Button blurted.

"No, Button. Don't do it," Mother pleaded.

Button reached deeply into her button purse and presented two of the stones.

"Mother, Providence has presented itself. It will not let you die. Here, let her go. You can have them. I have two," Button said as she stepped back a few paces, "Let her go. You can have them."

Mean's pouch reached for the two stones. Button kept offering hers as she continued to step back.

Mother's eyes brightened; she knew what Button was up to. She slightly nodded.

"Come get them," Button said.

But as soon as she said it, *PHHHT*. Button's stones flew to Mean's pouch. Button hustled aimlessly to the cave's rear wall. I assisted her.

Spewing out of the pool, the last commando miraculously landed in a ready position aiming his weapon at them.

"Where's the last stone?" Mean insisted.

Button shook her head and turned to Brob.

To the commando, Mean ordered, "Get the girl."

Brob leaped in front of him, which gave Button the time to reach out her left arm. The commando shifted, keeping Button at gunpoint. Brob growled. Button raised her hand.

"I want the last stone." Mean ordered. Mean's pouch reached toward Brob's belt. Brob's stone worked its way out and traveled slowly in mid-air toward Mean's. I tried to delay their joining, but the desire of the stones to be together remained a strong force. Mother glanced at Button. The commando switched his aim toward Brob. Brob smiled.

"Now, Button." Mother yelled out. Button slammed the Rock of Horeb with her hand.

Water gushed with a torrential force that catapulted the commando across the floor. Mother managed to slam her elbow into Mean, while Brob dove for the traveling stone. He got it.

"Nice stone. You stay here," Brob said as he put it back into his pouch.

In the distraction, Mother sucker-punched Mean and flipped him into the gushing stream. Mean unconsciously floated within the waves of gushing water. The commando sloshed through the torrent of water, trying to come to his aid.

After knowingly lifting a few things off the commando's belt while he tended Mean, Brob instructed the women, "Get to the container." Mother instantly grabbed Button and leaped into an opened one. Brob headed for the lever.

"Brob," shouted Button. The commando took aim.

Simultaneously, Brob pulled down the lever and shot off the grappling hook he had lifted from the commando; he immediately rose out of the commando's original sighting. The ladies traveled up within the tracking system.

BAM BAM BAM. The commando's aim wavered due to the gushing water now filling the floor of the cave, but Brob struggled. His weight had strained the grappling wire. Down he plummeted toward the commando, who still tried to shoot, but the Rock of Horeb would have nothing of it. It gushed more and changed its aim to disarm the man. Its discernment measured if Brob came down, he would need more water to break his fall. Unfortunately, the last shot of the commando snapped the tracking chain below the container Button and Mother were in. It set the container spinning as it rose.

Brob sloshed his way through the chest-high water to the rough-sided cave wall where the escape ladder hung high above the cave's floor. At this point, the water's level stood above Brob's head. The ladder, being custom built for giants like him, offered Brob his best exit. He began to scale the cave's wall toward the first lattice of the ladder.

The one remaining commando found Mean, still unconscious, floating by. He pulled a rip string on Mean's vest to inflate his floating device. Snatching Mean's holstered gun, he began shooting at Mother and Button.

Bullets ricocheted off the container. Mother reached around to close the container's door to protect them from the gunfire. "We're going to need to get this closed" Mother said. They observed the container's contents; golden crowns filled every empty space.

"Sir. Wake up, sir." The commando, after getting no response, slapped Mean hard. It took Mean a while to assess his surroundings, but he came out fighting. He thrashed for his grappling hook and grabbed the commando. Because of their weight, their ascent slow, but their direction stood the right course.

Brob had reached the ladder, which led to the escape tunnel to the next cave. Brob hustled as best he could; he knew they needed help.

"Oh, dear," Mother said.

"Throw some of this out so we can close this door," Button cried. Button laid hold of a scepter as they spun. She started to pitch it toward Mean when her Mother snatched it back.

"It's the golden scepter of Ahasuerus," she said.

PING BAM PING.

"Have you noticed they're SHOOTING AT US?" Button said as she picked up a large golden crown.

Even in the height of all this, Mother displayed her astonishing assertiveness for her daughter to see. She grabbed the crown away from Button.

"That's Mordecai's crown," Mother said.

Bullets ricocheted off the container. "They're mostly crowns, Mother. Something has to go." Button pleaded.

Mother started rooting through the container. She mumbled through her choice, "No, Queen Esther's."

Mean's approach crept toward them, but his bullets merely pinged on their spinning container. Button joined the search, and she and Mother simultaneously grabbed a crown.

"Queen Vashti's," they both cried out. Mother nabbed it and hurled it upward where it plunked Mean's grappling point of contact with the cave's ceiling. Mean and the commando plummeted into the deep water.

Brob, on the wall ladder just below the exit, yelled out, "Close the box, stand on it and swing to me."

Button looked up toward Brob and wondered if enough time remained to escape. They needed to decisively move toward that objective. Mother climbed the chain to close the door, but the door still jammed. A thin-ringed crown had lodged itself at the hinge. Mother tried to kick it out with no progress. Button joined in. "Where is Ayin when you need him?" Button muttered.

"Ayin? You have seen him?" Mother asked while continuing to

dislodge the door. Button nodded while yanking on it. "You should not speak so disrespectfully about him," Mother said.

"SWING to me. Forget it. Swing before it's too late."

Button and Mother started a bit of sway, but it wasn't enough.

"Climb down to the bottom of the chain, Mother. It'll help it swing," Button said as her Mother quickly complied. Like an excellent trapeze artist, she assisted the swinging greatly.

As it swung, Button began her descent down the chain. "Take Mother first, Brob."

"No," Mother yelled.

"Johnny Weissmuller, Brob. Johnny Weissmuller," Button yelled.

Brob's eyes brightened, then he let out a piercing Tarzan yell and catapulted to the oncoming swinging chain. Button smiled.

With one swing he had Mother in tow and perfectly tossed her to the landing of the exit's ledge. On the second swing, Brob gathered Button and launched her safely to her Mother's side. Brob let out another Tarzan yell and went for an extra swing, enjoying the acrobatics.

"Come on, Keeper," Mother urged.

"One more," Brob replied. With a loop-de-loop...NO. His stone fell out of his pouch.

It plummeted down, down, to the vast sea of water the Rock of Horeb unfurled, but the watchful eye of John Mean caught its approach.

"Oh, Mother," Button said in despair. She grabbed hold of her Mother and attempted to travel but she could not. Her efforts were not met with the necessary faith. Water remained an issue for Button.

Plop. The stone entered the water right in front of Mean.

Mean glanced up as Brob swung from the rising chain.

Mean plopped a portable air tank into his mouth and dove.

The commando kept surveying Brob.

"The Keeper is old," said Brob as he swung from the last remnants of the chain.

"The Keeper is not old. Come." Mother pleaded.

With a glance, Brob said, "Go." He dove for the water below as the last opened container and its crowns crashed through the exit.

Button screamed, "NO."

CHAPTER 15

SPIRITUAL WARFARE

ON THE NAVIGATIONAL DECK, the orphans gathered around Brob's map with Father. Father looked ridiculous with Hue's scarves pinned to portions of his body, but he couldn't risk losing all from Mean's book. As it stood, this allowed him to retain only a portion.

"Pirate, put us ashore on this small beach, there," Father said as he pointed to it exactly. "The right containers track to the exit right by this beach."

"Right containers?" Hazel asked.

Father traced the elaborate tracking system on the map. "It's an ingenious layout of subterfuge. Trust me, these are the containers you'll want to hook to."

Hazel pitched her five invented tow clips to Fish. "When we beach, just slap them on, and they'll automatically insert."

"Got it," said Fish.

"The rest of you will have to crank those heavy containers to the beach's edge. I imagine it'll take all your strength, but it must be done," instructed Father, "Now scatter and detach all chains and ropes you can use in your assignment."

The orphans dispersed.

"What about you?" Hazel asked as she pointed to the map marked by a snake, "Got any ideas?"

"I do," Father responded with a sly smile. "The real containers are right here."

Hazel pointed to containers at the beach exit. "Subterfuge, indeed. I think I know what you're up to."

* * *

AMIDST THE DARKNESS AND SHADOWS, Mother groped the side of the new cave's wall.

"We must go back," Button pleaded.

"It's somewhere around here, I believe," Mother mumbled.

"He'll drown," Button exclaimed with tears forming.

"There," Mother said and with a yank. SNAP. Revolving lights, like a disco ball, flew over Button.

They could hear a faint, distant hiss, and as Button turned around, she saw King Francis's formal hanging from the cave's ceiling. Beams of light reflected off the thirteen thousand buttons on the garment. Button allowed herself the time to gaze upon it. Her mind whirled for it seemed intact. The depth of her Mother's love touched her. Obviously, Mother's desire to present it to her after she found it had not come. But this minute presentation didn't cover what Button thought it would be.

Mother locked arms with Button. "Hurry, dear." She hustled her down the long descending stoned pathway to the cave's floor.

"King Francis's formal. You found it."

"Yes, yes, years ago."

"And you never told me?"

"Your eighteenth birthday–that's what it is for. It's safe where it is. Believe me."

The lights slightly brightened again.

"In a damp cave?" Button questioned.

"Hazel put a protective coating on it. Hurry, Button."

"Mother, we must go back for Brob," Button insisted.

Mother stopped momentarily, searching both sides of the steps. "The Keeper will come," Mother said as she took a couple more steps, searching.

"How do you know this?"

"The Keeper has lived a long time. He knows how to survive."

"But, Mother," Button protested.

Mother grabbed her and faced off, "Sometimes difficult decisions need to be made, my precious."

The lights brightened again. Button noticed this time.

"What's happening?" she asked.

"Quickly, the coating turns the reflections of the buttons to lasers," Mother said as she waved her closer. She pushed a stone, and a secret compartment opened. Multiple mirror discs were inside. Mother gathered them quickly. "Grab my waist and stay close behind me. Mirror my every step."

A beam of light from the formal slightly burned Button's shoulder.

"Ouch." Button flinched.

Mother situated six of the mirror discs in her suit. She rethought her decision and put two back into the secret compartment, closing it.

Button, at Mother's waist, saw the long pathway ahead of them to a wide slate-rocked ledge before the exit of the cave.

Mother pushed forward while juggling the discs, reflecting the now deadly beams from hitting them.

FATHER, Hazel, and the orphans finally anchored Mean's yacht off the correct shore. They disembarked and navigated a rubberized engine powered raft up to the slate rock ramp, the back entrance to the final cave.

As they trekked up, they could see the exposed containers on their tracking system at an exposed opening in the rocks. A dismantled cranking apparatus sat at the water's edge. Fish, Chef,

Pirate, and Cowboy, carrying ropes, went directly to it to figure out its operation. The found the crank device folded and in need of assembly; unfortunately, each of the boys had a different idea on how to construct it. Intermittent spats ensued.

Fish had enough. "I'll hook the ropes to the boat," he said. "Help me tie them, Chef."

"No, no, no," Pirate said, "I know knots. They have to be the right knots."

Chef and Cowboy hovered over the crank device, still puzzled.

"Maybe this," said Cowboy. What he built resembled a mechanical bull.

"No, no, no," Chef said as he swiftly dismantled it and built the apparatus into something that looked like a giant Foley Food Mill. "It's like this."

"Hurry Willow," said Hazel, "The fact that those containers are exposed indicates they've been evacuating the caves. If they get to the last one before you…"

Father became worried.

"Go. Go. We've got this." Hazel said.

Father rushed to the entrance. "Keep to the plan, Hazel. Don't risk the children." He disappeared into the cave's entrance.

"I won't," Hazel called back and turned to assist the boys when suddenly she noticed Hue halfway up to the cave.

"Hue, honey. This way," Hazel said, but Hue stood peering into the cave.

"He's in trouble. The giant; he's in trouble," said Hue.

Hazel gently swung around and approached her, kneeling to embrace her. "I know you have a special place for him, Hue. The Keeper has lived a long time. We must trust he's all right and capable."

"Yes, Ma'am," Hue quietly responded and accompanied Hazel to the task at hand. But after giving a hint as to the crank's construction to Cowboy and Chef, Hazel panicked.

Hue had disappeared.

* * *

THE DARK, dim pathways of the cave were perplexing to Father, but haste overcame his inquisitiveness. He flashed his light on the tunnel's walls. He tripped (a habit of his in his preoccupation).

"No time for that, Willow," he said as he flashed his light down the tunnel. It revealed a sharp bend in the pathway.

"Yes, yes. This is it."

Father rushed to the bend, took five paces around it and shined his light upon the wall overhead. A rectangular rock formation hung from the top. A horizontal line in the ceiling by the wall's edge gave him the clue he needed. He quickly aligned himself under the line, flattened himself against the wall and felt for something.

His left hand moved over one rock, then another, then to a third rock. He simultaneously stomped the ground and slammed the rock and BOOM. The rock formation fell to the ground, forming a stairway to the ceiling.

Father flashed his light up. There stood the container with the snake staff engraved on its exterior. Father rushed up the rock stairs. "This was destroyed. You know this Willow" he mumbled to himself. "She'll know it too. But here it is." Father looked up. "Please let this instill faith."

* * *

MOTHER, with all her motor skills, reflected the laser beams with the mirrors—a slow-moving process for her and Button. But the rotation of the cloak increased, and the onslaught of beams escalated.

"Now comes the hard part," Mother said.

The hissing sound resounded no longer distant. Snakes came out of the opening corridors of the exit. Mother rerouted around them and zapped them with her juggling act, redirecting each beam at a snake, obliterating it.

"Snakes? You didn't say anything about snakes," Button gasped.

Mother, juggling her four specialized mirrors, let one drop behind them, so its reflection smoked a sneaky snake.

"Not just snakes, Button. They're deadly vipers," Mother said as she double-timed it now that she only had three mirrors.

"I can travel." Button confessed, suddenly.

"I know."

"You know?"

"If you can; do it."

Button squeezed her eyes shut. "This never works when I want it to." Try as she might, they went nowhere.

"Behind you. Catch this." Mother flipped a mirror to her.

I couldn't help myself. I acted without permission. Time slowed for Button. Oblivious to my help, she caught the mirror and turned to see an oversized viper about to strike from behind. Before fear could reach her, she perceived a beam coming toward her and had enough time to correctly waylay the beam's path to smite the viper. I was satisfied with my decision for Button wasn't the juggler like her Mother.

Button reached the mirror over her mother's shoulder, and Mother quickly incorporated it into her elaborate choreography.

"This is fantastical," Button whimpered as she tripped slightly and splashed some water on her rebound.

"Stay with me, Button. Almost there," Mother said as she exterminated more vipers down the path.

Slosh, slosh. Button looked back and saw water coming down from the steps. Following its source up to the stairs, she could see Mean pointing his weapon at Brob.

"It's Brob," Button shouted.

Mother glanced but got zapped on the ankle by a beam.

"Aww."

Mean descended the stairs with Brob ahead of him.

Mother limped and struggled to keep the zaps and snakes off them until…

"Over here, Mother," Father called beyond them.

"Father." Button cried out as she peered down the pathway.

Father stood before the opened serpent container, scarves and all, with the serpent staff.

"Look, Mother," Button instructed. "Look toward Father."

Struggling in her own effort, Mother could not pull herself away from saving herself and her daughter.

"I can't, Button," she said.

"But we can," said Button as she grabbed her Mother's head and forced her to focus ahead. "Ayin. Do you see him?"

Ayin held sentry on the other side of the container behind Father.

Mother squinted. "The divine light is here?"

"Cast your eyes on the staff. Keep them there," Father instructed.

Ayin touched the serpent staff, and it emitted a staggering light. By his mere presence, pathways of light sprung before them, clearing the vipers and the beams.

"He's right in front of us. See the pathway?"

Mother abandoned her mirrors and focused on the staff, for she had the faith that Ayin's presence existed even though she couldn't see him.

Button assisted her mother with her limp, as they picked up their pace.

* * *

SURPRISINGLY, I received instructions to leave my protégé'. The order emitted great reluctance within me, but I knew it must have been of great importance.

There I stood, illuminating a dark caverned tunnel that contained the exiting containers from the tracking system. I heard a distant humming. I knew her arrival was imminent, but I didn't approach. I enlightened the way for her so fear would not encapsulate her. Hue stopped when my brightness stood too much for her. I toned it down.

"I am Samandiriel. Where are you going, little warrior?" I asked.

"I'm going to find the giant," she responded as she curiously assessed me, amazingly with no fear.

"It is not your task at this time to assist."

Hue bowed her head in discernment and asked, "He has help?"

"He has always had help; his time is not his. Providence will meet your friend, the giant," I responded.

"You mean he's in God's hands?" she asked.

I hadn't felt such endearment in a long time, marveling how she could know at such a small age. "You must go back, little warrior."

Hue yawned and sighed. Oftentimes the gifts of the Spirit are strongest during the twilight stages of sleep.

"You must return the way you came. The others are worried about you," I insisted.

Hue looked behind her. "Will you light the way?"

"Give me one of your scarves," I said.

When she obliged, I swept it up and wrapped such an illumination within its fabric that the blessing of it would last for years. I tossed it in the air for her to catch and then I flew through the tunnel.

Hue smiled and turned to go back. She yawned. I softly spoke behind her, "Stay awake, little warrior."

Hue walked off tossing her illumining scarf up, lighting the way as she went. Even as I tarried, I could hear Hazel's faint yet frantic call for her. She would be fine.

* * *

Brob stood opposite the exit's ledge at the beginning of the long corridor. He existed completely and totally resigned to serving Mean, now the holder of the five stones.

"Get me over there," Mean commanded.

"I cannot," Brob responded.

"You have the power. Now do it." Mean shouted.

"I do not ride Holy Wind."

"I, the holder of the stones, your ancestor, say you do." Mean insisted as he held the stone's pouch tightly and dramatically reached to touch Brob.

After a long pause...

"I do not ride Holy Wind," Brob repeated as he opened Mother's secret compartment. Disheartened, he snatched the two remaining mirrors. "Get on back. We go."

Mean complied after Brob kneeled solemnly.

"But my book. I'm sure it is you."

"Nope, not me."

At the end of the long corridor, Button and Mother lurched forward in a mad dash toward Father as Ayin waived the serpent container closed. Father pulled his family from the ledge's edge, looking up saying, "Thank you, thank you."

Stopping short of embracing Father, Button sensed something wrong as she glanced behind. "Brob," she screamed. Father and Mother snatched her back as the serpent container tracked away.

To Father, Mother asked, "Did you push something?"

Father shook his head.

"Why is it tracking away?" said Mother.

Father shrugged.

"It found no faith," Button whispered. "The Keeper feels old."

Button eyed Brob and Mean as they started through the viper's corridor. Hearing a whoosh, Button whipped around.

Ayin stood face to face with her.

"I'm right, aren't I? That's why I can't travel at will. My being sees the danger, and my faith flees."

Mother whispered to Father. "Who's she whispering to? Do you see him?" She attempted to retrieve Button, but Father held her back.

"No, but it doesn't mean there isn't someone there," Father whispered back.

"It must be Ayin." Mother started to kneel.

Father whispered back, "Stand up, woman, it's not the Lord. Besides, history has the snake staff destroyed. That's a fake. Something or someone heavenly empowered it."

"Brob put it back together?" Mother said.

"I don't know why," Father said. "But I do know it's served its purpose. Its removal has forced Button into her epiphany."

"She looked at Ayin, not the staff. The staff was for me. And what exactly is her purpose?" Mother asked.

Father took her hand and responded, "To set the captive free. Watch."

Button boldly circled Ayin, conversing as to the air. "The Keeper feels old. He won't make it. You must do something, Ayin, he has lost his faith."

"Your imagination empowers you, yet you are a young warrior," Ayin simply said. "You see what can be, but still lack."

Button squinted. "Where's the profundity in that?" Ayin smiled greatly. Button tried to break through her puzzlement as she saw Brob take zap after zap from the vipers and lasers.

"Oh. I found faith in my imagination but have not applied it to the person that I really am," Button whispered.

Button rushed to the ledge's end. Mother cried out after her, but Father said, "I've read Ma'mah's book, remember. Let her go. Faith expects action. It's what her imagination taught her: bravery, compassion, endurance..."

As the vipers relentlessly bit Brob, Button reached for her purse but suddenly ceased. She stretched out her arms toward Brob, and she softly prayed, "Help me in my unbelief." *Whoosh!* Button swiftly rode the Holy Wind and enveloped Brob in her travel. Mean barely maintained his piggy-back ride, clasping onto Brob's shirt.

KAPLOP. The force of her travel produced a rough landing for them; they skidded down the lengthy rock ledge toward the cave's opening. Coming to a halt, Brob turned on his back in his weakness, breathing heavily. Mother rushed to his side.

Mean groped to his feet and peered at Button. He charged

Button in his great anger and revelation. Father once again had to hold Mother back.

"Treasure, no," Mother groaned.

"Be at peace, my love, and see the wonders to come," he smiled.

Button held her ground, squinting and fidgeting in great anticipation. I stood at a full height right behind her with Ayin.

"It's you. It's you who has the power." Mean shouted.

Ayin stepped out and stood between the two. Mean squirmed, not seeing Ayin's presence. Ayin finger-flicked Mean's nose (something I've never seen him do; he seemed to enjoy it.). As Mean jerked back and flinched around looking for someone, Father stepped forward.

"I have a proposition," Father said.

Ignoring him, Mean walked a full circle around Button, squirming somewhat, trying to shake off Ayin's presence.

"Your boat is out there," said Father as he pointed toward the exit. "All the artifact canisters are hooked to it. You leave now, and there will be no trouble."

Mother called out as she went back to attend Brob, "The stones."

"Yes, yes, you will need to give me the stones."

Mean sneered at Father. With his power and a mere wave of his hand, he sent Father sliding on the cave's floor, landing next to Mother.

"Still feeling confident, Treasure?" Mother asked.

Ayin advanced upon Mean; Button stood her ground. The violation against her father filled her with righteous anger.

Mean took a step back before his whole demeanor encompassed the evil within him. Then, he stepped forward. "You don't want to mess with me," he proclaimed.

Declaration had been made, and there would be conflict, so our full appearance was commanded. I appeared on Button's left, Ayin on her right. Mother gasped, and Father halfway smiled, despite his head injury.

Button's hand went into her button purse then hesitated.

Ayin turned toward her with a 'go-ahead' smile and asked, "Are you in the Grace of God?"

She reached deep into her button purse. "If I am not, may God put me there, and if I am, may God so keep me." She leaned in toward Mean and proclaimed. "No, sir, you don't want to mess with the power that fuels me."

As all looked on, Button transformed into Joan of Arc in full battle array. Mother tried to speak, but all utterance escaped her. Father blurted, "There's some confidence."

Button whooshed around Mean. Every time he attempted to grab her, she traveled to the next point. Her next pass ripped the pouch of stones from his belt, and she immediately heaved it toward Mother.

The stone-filled pouch bonked Mother on the head, for she stayed too stunned at what she saw to catch it. It bounced off her for the perfect reception; Father managed to catch the pouch despite his seemingly inebriated condition.

"Flee now and take what we've offered," Button commanded.

Mean braced himself and slapped his hands downward to allow the powers of the legion within him to culminate. Power waves emitted below him, and as he raised his hands, their emission intensified into a whirling portal for evil. Dark mist, forming shapes of earthly elements, came through. They were fire, strong wind, cold ice, and water.

As Ayin hurried to Button's side, he said, "Do not let him touch you. You are young." She felt strong, but her nod showed reluctance. "Look behind you," Ayin added.

The light rays of several Principalities stood ready for their orders. Their vast color arrays illuminated the cave with vivid colors (not normally seen by Earth Dwellers since the fall of man).

"Principalities. Can Mean see them?" Button whispered to Ayin.

"He senses some presence but no, not at this time. Your entourage, however, does see them, their faith has allowed it.

They are chosen. He is not. They will be ordered if needed." As Ayin spoke, he retreated before the evil powers.

Mean, thinking he could get the jump on Button, waved the four elements to surround her. Button, with great skill, sliced the ice into splinters with her sword, deflected the fire by fragmenting it into several pieces and then sent the fire to melt the remaining ice. Then, she rerouted the wind with her shield to extinguish each of the flames.

Ayin and I shared a smile, for we noted Button's physical fight became intuitive. Her Father's brilliance had finally passed down to his daughter, after years of her desperately wanting to follow in her mother's footsteps. She now understood righteous authority offered wisdom in all situations. A quick glance toward Father supported our conclusion; tears dropped from his eyes, tears of fulfillment. But the next obstacle to defeat was water.

Button let the wave chase her as she thought of a plan. The Principalities moved forward, anxious to set righteousness in place. Without turning, Ayin just flipped up his hand. They halted obediently, for they knew they would have to answer to him if they disobeyed. Ayin then nodded to me.

Immediately, my radiance stood before Father and Mother. "She practices your wisdom, but she still needs your wisdom, and you need not to rely on it by itself. Sometimes things get physical." Even though Father stood there perplexed, I knew he'd figure it out; otherwise, the order from Ayin would have never come.

Father watched Button being chased by the water.

The wave grew and caught Button off guard. Her shield could not hold it, and the end portion of the wave shifted to attack her from the opposite side. "Make it rain," Father shouted up at her. With split-second thinking, Button traveled through the wave, separating portions of the water with her shield in front of her. Wielding her sword like a master samurai, she split the separated waves into tiny rain droplets while holding off the main flow with her shield. Repeatedly, she separated and chopped until it disintegrated.

With a nod from Ayin, the Principalities changed the consistency of the water by emitting a soft, gentle wind; the rain became light healing waters for those below. Father's head trauma cleared, Mother's laser-burnt legs healed, and Brob revived enough to sit up.

Button hovered over Mean and shouted, "Where is your sting when the Lord has shown Himself?"

Mean's furious anger fueled the portal. It enlarged and released massive quantities of evil spirits.

Ayin immediately waved in the Principalities and Powers. Three transformed into the Angels of Birth and Death; others remained in the form of the holy mist and lights. Ayin commanded a few angelic color-shifting Thrones toward Father and Mother. Their wheel-within-a-wheel shape darted anxiously before their charges. Their many eyes served as an early warning for the oncoming and as clues for how their charges should attack.

Ugliness sprang from the portal, taking the form of beasts with armor. Button slaughtered them into nothingness as they surfaced, but the onslaught became too heavy for her. The colorful powers of the Angels of Birth and Death flew to Button's side in full battle array. They fought with all their might.

One beefy looking angel enjoyed pouncing and squashing his opponent, and another robust angel caught many with a leap, gripping them within his legs and sending them into a tailspin before they dissipated. A third angel had beauty beyond compare; she enticed the ugliness to their doom; about the moment they would embrace her, she would pounce on them with all the ugliness they represented, leaving them trapped in a barrier the form of a transparent cubed block. Button, as she fought, would slice them into nothing.

Ayin and I still held back, but I managed a piercing glance toward Father. He stood there staring at the eyes of a Throne who attempted to warn him of an oncoming evil spirit resembling an ancient martial arts expert.

Forcefully, the spirit karate-chopped Father to the ground. The Thrones enveloped his arms and legs to assist as he leaped up in his righteous anger.

"I think you need more Yangs to go with your Yin. A lot more." Father, with the aid of the Thrones, engaged in a sparring match between the two no one could have imagined. Such leaps, such kicks, such acrobatics. But what almost made me giggle were all the reminder scarves Hue had attached to his body. They made his flowing moves delightfully humorous.

Watching the fight, Mother got caught off guard by an incoming forceful giant and he pummeled her to the ground. Beautifully choreographed her arm when up and caught the stone pouch Father had thrown to her while the spherical lights of her Thrones enveloped her arms and legs. The stones escaped their pouch and dropped right into her hands. She hammered the giant to the ground by juggling the stones with great expertise and speed.

When both Father and Mother had their opponents submissively kneeling, they stopped their assault, simultaneously whacked them once, and said, "By His power, go away." Their opponents dissolved. Mother picked up the pouch and secured the stones.

Satisfied with their efforts, Mother and Father embraced, but a swift mist of a tiny spirit snatched the stone pouch. Its teasing zigzag motion eluded Mother and Father as they tried to retrieve it.

Brob did not tolerate mockery well. Being revived, he marched to Mother and Father and roared his loudest toward the teasing spirit. When a giant roars, well... the tiny spirit trembled a bit then popped out of existence, leaving the pouch to dangle momentarily before falling.

Brob tried to catch the pouch, but another evil spirit quickly raced away with it and returned it to Mean. He turned to Mother and Father, who were flattened to the ground by his roar. He helped them to stand and addressed the Principalities, "FIGHT. They are too much for her. You must get them back."

Ayin waved the Principalities into the skirmish. They took on the appearance of brightly colored Guardian Angels and dispersed to aid all who were trying to help Button. Some of the evil disbanded with the remnant of wind the flap of their wings released. The spread of their reach formed an impenetrable shield around Mother, Father, and Brob.

This battle became a sensory overload for the humans. Even though there are moments in time for God's people to view battles they are not easily assimilated. For us, our purpose to serve the command of the One and Only and aid His faithful servants — it always presents itself as a battleground. At this moment, all the evil abandoned everyone except Button. Everyone stood helpless to aid her.

She shielded, jabbed with her sword, kicked with her legs, but she barely survived the bombardment. Fear and doubt tried to take her as they pushed her down toward the ground to the awaiting Mean. His pompous smile infuriated us all. The entourage all wanted to rush to her aid, but their guardians would not let them.

Mean held the stones in one hand and reached his other toward the approaching Button. When he was about to touch her, Button came to an epiphany; she really didn't need a button. She swooped her hands to envelope the Holy Wind and pushed it towards Mean. We rejoiced. Her gift had progressed.

BAM. A powerful grand burst of light waved through the room, jettisoning most of the evil spirits into nothingness and catapulted Mean toward the exit. The stone pouch conveniently landed in Father's hands.

Mean gathered himself and stumbled toward the exit but to our surprise, Hue had entered. She stood before the light of the exit all silhouetted in her beauty. A magnificent halo outlined her figure giving her a sense of radiance. She remained a mighty infant warrior. Ayin and I swiftly made our way behind her but again, I was surprised. Ayin had something magnificent in mind, for he did not immediately assist her.

Father stood amazed, taking it all in.

Back to her normal self, Button pursued Mean, but Father called her softly. "Wait, Button."

"But the artifacts?"

"They're fine. They're safe," Father said as he gazed endearingly yet puzzled toward Hue.

A clandestine spirit advanced toward Hue but she was not taken off guard. She nonchalantly threw my scarf at it. POOF. The spirit disappeared. I believe this was part of Ayin's anticipation.

Enraptured in all of this, Mother had crept forward. "Hue, honey, come." Father gently coaxed Mother back.

Momentarily Mean's eyes soften as he drew nearer to Hue. We heavenlies weren't expecting this but it led us to suspect that Ayin did.

As Mean wobbled forward he asked, "Are you mine?"

"I belong to only one." Hue replied.

"And who might that be?"

"The righteous one who begot me."

The legion remaining in Mean would have none of it. Mean pressed forward and retorted, "I think your mother has kept you from me.

Mean reached for Hue; Ayin swiftly held his hand of protection over her. He tempered the orchestration of the ill-advised boldness within her and she followed Ayin's lead by walking a couple of steps toward Mean. He was about to touch her.

"Come with me. I'll show you much." Mean doubled over as he met my thrown scarf again. Hue was small, but no feeble. The spirits that no longer wished to remain within Mean exited causing him great anguish.

Hazel rushed in from the exit behind Hue screaming, "No! Hue, honey, come to me. John, leave now, leave before you—"

"Tell him, Mother. It is time." Hue's simple statement shocked them all.

Reluctantly, Hazel approached Hue's side; she had a great sense of puniness wave over her; fear had gripped her. The orphans tried to follow her entrance, but Hazel "shushed" them back behind the cleft. All the secret guilt and sorrow surfaced on Hazel's face. Her momentary gaze toward her sister was met with Mother's compassionate countenance.

Face to face with Mean, as Hue still played with her scarf, Hazel pleaded.

"John, I know you're in there somewhere. Please don't take her. Find the mercy you once had." Hazel begged, but I knew she would not find what she sought. John Mean obeyed the legion within him for many years. Just when I thought all hope for him was gone, his eyes, for a moment, turned the beautiful green they once were and looked at Hue with endearment. But just as quickly as it came, it escaped him; he grabbed for Hue, but Ayin's hand swiftly jerked her away.

In the presence of Ayin's holiness, Hazel stooped frozen to the ground. Father and Mother swiftly gathered her behind Brob. But the orphans felt the draw of the present holiness and their increased curiosity drew them into the cave. I rushed to their protecting, herding them toward the group behind Brob.

"Stop pushing me," Pirate said.

"It isn't me," retorted Chef.

They could not see our presence. At what would seem the most inopportune time, I smiled. Yes, illumination pursued so I thought to make a partial appearance to set them still for what was about to come. Of course, they pulled back.

"You can't stop me," Mean said as he approached Hue. Every ounce of the remaining legion sequestered the fight to remain with the living.

"Yes, we can." At that proclamation, Button traveled toward Hue gathering a large amount of Holy Wind. Simultaneously, it struck Mean as Hue's scarf let loose its own large wave of righteousness. As the wave enveloped Mean's head, his very shape distorted as the ugly tormenting spirits fled his body.

"Fight, Daddy. Fight for your freedom." Hue barked, unafraid of the evacuation.

Screaming spirits fled and tried to enter others that were there. At their commanded dissipation, we heavenlies made sure none free to enter anyone else there. Mean's convulsions had taken him to the ground, but the legion's last efforts elevated him.

Button would have none of it. All that remained in Mean must be liberated. She traveled upward right with him gathering once again the Holy Wind. She could see the shadow of Hue's outreached arm on the ceiling of the cave about to reach Mean.

By instinctual wisdom, Brob braced before the entourage. I, too, stood beside him.

When Hue's shadow touched the tip of Mean's form, Button's thrust of Holy Wind met Mean. He contorted so violently that his body thrashed off the walls. We could barely track his trail; the movement was lightning fast but Brob's roar and my illumination sent him flying when his trajectory headed for the orphans.

Ayin had seen enough. He removed his hand from over Hue and swept a motion to Mean that catapulted him out of the cave.

With a swift sense of maternal love, Button scooped Hue up and traveled out the exit.

CHAPTER 16

BUTTON RETURNS HOME

I, OF COURSE, MET THEM AS they landed hard on the exterior slated rock.

"Where did he go?" asked Button

"He's on his boat," I replied.

Hue, with her compassionate eyes, muttered, "Will he come back?"

"The legion is swept clean; he must replace the space, or they will return.

Brob, Mother, Father and the orphans made their way down the ledge. Hazel breached the exit first just to be sure Hue was well. When she turned to check on the orphans behind her guilt remained prevalent even though it had been forgiven long ago. Mother's endearing smile and soft hand lifted Hazel's head and without any hesitation, they embraced.

Hazel blurted, "We've had another adventure."

Mother responded, "We've had an adventure doing the Lord's work."

As all began to congregate, Hue walked up to her mother interrupting her hug.

139

Within all her blubbering, Hazel managed to say, "Hue, this is your Auntie."

Mother embraced Hue as Brob belted, "Little One." Hue hugged Brob's shin with an endless grip.

"There, little one, I'm fine."

"Look," Pirate said as the containers started to pull away one after another.

"No, the artifacts," Mother shouted.

Father whipped her around in his arms and said, "They're all decoys, my love."

"What?" Mother asked.

Brob patted his chest with great satisfaction, "Brob skilled in subterfuge."

Like a proud parent, Father patted the orphans on the back and proclaimed, "Job well-done crew."

"What happened in there?" asked Pirate.

Fished asked, "Did you see that bright smiling woman?"

The orphans gathered around Button and rehashed their part in the quest as Father linked arms with Mother and swung her aside and said, "You know, Mean has a book, too."

"Nyoo!"

"Yes, it's all here," Father said as he indicated all the various sized scarves attached to his body.

"I wondered about their pertinence. I know you're not prone to play."

"What? Play? Look at all this. Certainly, it displays a bit of play?"

"Treasure, the book?"

"Yes, yes, we can't flip our book until its ready, but when I flipped his book, I couldn't remember what the previous page said. So, Hue suggested using her scarves as tools to remember. It's quite ingenious. The clues they represent are all here; now I just have to glean what the clues mean," Father said as he staged his scarf presentation. "This is kind of fun."

"Willow," Hazel complained.

"You said I didn't play; I play," Father said.

"Treasure, get it out," Mother encouraged.

As he took off the scarf around his bicep, he explained, "It said the surviving giant remained empowered. Mean misinterpreted it. You see, Meshel Stehl is the only reference in our book. The Moabite and the Canaanite language can be confusing. He believed the Moabitess transferred this power to Brob; therefore, Brob could transfer it to him. The empowerment the book really stated was Brob is no longer a pagan. He walks in the power of the Chosen One as the Moabitess did. Now the power to travel like Philip the Evangelist did, that has been gifted to our dear Button."

"Yes, I've seen that. And what do those two represent?" Mother asked as she snickered and pointed to the two scarves attached to his loin area.

"I'll have to think about those. At another time, perhaps?"

"Another time?" Mother asked.

"Next time, we do this together." Father smiled and embraced Mother briefly. "I do know what this one is." He held up his three fingers tied together with a tiny, thin scarf. "There are three particular artifacts that need to be freed. The stones being one of them. There existed a slight indication the possessor of all three might receive some power, but again, all the pages aren't coming to me." He gazed at all the scarves on his body. "But it will. Hey, you've retained all I've told you, right?"

Mother nodded, perplexed.

"Good, then I can remove these." He untied the tiny one around his fingers and the one on his bicep. Then he handed the stones to Mother and nodded toward Brob.

"It's time," Father said.

Mother, with great formality, approached Brob with her hand outstretched.

"Brob, I, the descendant of the Moabitess, release you from your servitude. You are free to go and be the Keeper."

An unexpected wind rushed around Brob. The orphans

stopped their jabbering with Button and turned to see. Brob reached for the stone's pouch and one by one, the stones traveled out of the pouch into Brob's hand. Fully refreshed, Brob rose to his full height looking youthful. Button scanned the area, and there Ayin stood at the cave's entrance.

Button smiled dearly toward Ayin. Reviving the aging giant blessed her. Her attachment to him had grown strong. She understood Ayin's encouragement to go home, for her body swayed with weakness from maintaining her inaugural travel time. Yet, all she wanted to do linger and smile at their wonderful faces. The love among them—her mother and father, Aunt Hazel and the orphans, Hue and Brob—it blessed her.

Then, Ayin nodded her toward her parents. Button walked to them and embraced them both.

Whoosh!

AT THE GARDEN TABLE AT THE Willow estate, Connor vigilantly hovered over Button, who still slept on the book.

Father and Mother, refreshed and changed, exited out of the broken library window.

"Glad to see you without your scarves," Mother teased.

"The photographs will do, thank you for helping," Father responded.

"I wish I could have seen this," Mother said, indicating the window.

"The boxing pages just flashed before me," Father replied.

"Truly a gift, Treasure," Mother said as she kissed him.

Father spoke to Connor, "How is she?"

"Not a stir, sir."

"She must be exhausted," Mother said.

Mother and Father knelt before Button. Father stroked Button's hair back as she slightly stirred.

"Mother?"

"Yes, Button, I'm home."

"Oh, Mother." Button arose and embraced her in her bewilderment. "Oh, dear, Father, you're quite a writer."

"It all happened, Button. Everything was real."

Button silently processed what her Father said. She succumbed to the reality of it all. But it was as if a person stood back from a picture they painted and thought, *there is no contemplation or fact that could have justified that I did this.*

"Brob? He's all right?"

"Yes, yes, the Keeper is well. Go with Mother, Button. You need to rest."

Mother led her off, but Button hesitated.

"There will be plenty of time for answers," Father said as she walked off with Mother.

"Next time, we use all our gifts together," Father called after her.

"Yes, Father. Good idea."

Mother smiled and escorted Button through the broken window.

"Oh, Mother, Father fought those men and..."

"...yes, dear, he told me all about it."

"How long have I been asleep?" Button asked.

"Since we returned, a few hours, that's all. Come."

They exit.

Father addressed Connor. "That will be all for the day. I thank you for your devotion, Connor."

"Yes, sir." Connor started to exit but turned back and asked. "Can the day be explained at some point, sir?"

"It may take more days experiencing such oddities first, Connor," Father answered.

"Good night, sir."

"Good night, Connor."

Father plopped down in front of the table with the opened leather book, contemplating.

"Perhaps another page?" Father whispered.

He flipped a page of the leather-bound book.

THE END

145

ABOUT THE AUTHOR

KIM P. WELLS resides in rural Missouri with her husband, Bob. During their thirty-five-years of marriage, they've homeschooled and raised eight children on their homestead and now greet new grandchildren yearly. Kim is a produced and an award-winning screenwriter. She looks forward to at least two more Button Willow episodes. Her intent with this series is to remind the public that the true origin of supernatural powers is GOD.

* * *

Catch us on www.facebook.com/buttonwillownovel for comments and Button Willow's updates.